Get Your
Coventry Romances
Home Subscription NOW

And Get These
4 Best-Selling Novels
FREE:

LACEY
by Claudette Williams

THE ROMANTIC WIDOW
by Mollie Chappell

HELENE
by Leonora Blythe

THE HEARTBREAK TRIANGLE

D1315197

A Home Subscription! It's the easiest and most convenient way to get every one of the exciting Coventry Romance Novels! ...And you get 4 of them FREE!

You pay nothing extra for this convenience: there are no additional charges...you don't even pay for postage! Fill out and send us the handy coupon now, and we'll send you 4 exciting Coventry Romance novels absolutely FREE!

SEND NO MONEY, GET THESE
FOUR BOOKS FREE!

CO481

**MAIL THIS COUPON TODAY TO:
COVENTRY HOME
SUBSCRIPTION SERVICE
6 COMMERCIAL STREET
HICKSVILLE, NEW YORK 11801**

YES, please start a Coventry Romance Home Subscription in my name, and send me FREE and without obligation to buy, my 4 Coventry Romances. If you do not hear from me after I have examined my 4 FREE books, please send me the 6 new Coventry Romances each month as soon as they come off the presses. I understand that I will be billed only $11.70 for all 6 books. There are no shipping and handling nor any other hidden charges. There is no minimum number of monthly purchases that I have to make. In fact, I can cancel my subscription at any time. The first 4 FREE books are mine to keep as a gift, even if I do not buy any additional books.

For added convenience, your monthly subscription may be charged automatically to your credit card.

☐ Master Charge ☐ Visa

Credit Card # _____

Expiration Date _____

Name _____
(Please Print)

Address _____

City _____ State _____ Zip _____

Signature _____

☐ Bill Me Direct Each Month

This offer expires Dec. 31, 1981. Prices subject to change without notice. Publisher reserves the right to substitute alternate FREE books. Sales tax collected where required by law. Offer valid for new members only.

PERDITA

a novel by

Joan Smith

FAWCETT COVENTRY • NEW YORK

PERDITA

Published by Fawcett Coventry Books, a unit of CBS
Publications, the Consumer Publishing Division of CBS Inc.

Copyright © 1981 by Joan Smith

ISBN: 0-449-50173-6

Printed in the United States of America

First Fawcett Coventry printing: April 1981

10 9 8 7 6 5 4 3 2 1

PERDITA

Chapter One

No woman wants to be plain, but I am fast coming to the conclusion that to be *too* beautiful is almost worse. I am not plagued by any excess of beauty myself. It is that of my charge, Perdita, that caused us all the trouble. She is an exquisite little thing, like a blond, dimpled angel from an old painting breathed into life. She is dainty of stature, though her body is very well filled out for a lady of seventeen years. Besides being young and beautiful, she is possessed of an embarrassingly large fortune. One cannot outline her situation without realizing she is a tailor-made heroine. She has a stepmother wicked enough to be pushing an unwanted match on her, a father too obedient to his new wife to say no, and before we had gone ten miles on our journey, she also had a rake hounding her. I ought really to be evil as well to complete her case, but I hope I am not. There is just one other thing lacking: a heroine ought, by rights, to be a biddable creature. Perdita, as you will see, is nothing of the sort.

My father was an army man. He adhered to the military principle of getting over heavy ground as light as you can. Well then, here is the background to the tale. I jawed Perdita's father, Sir Wilfrid Brodie, into letting me take Perdita for a visit to her aunt when she dug in her heels and called her suitor an old goat, to his face. Sir Wilfrid, being no fool, felt a short absence was the best way to bring Mr. Croft back to his former state of infatuation. Lady Brodie agreed, because all she really wanted was such youthful competition as Perdita out of her house. Naturally it was her mother's sister, Mrs. Cosgrove, I had in mind, but in a fit of paternal propriety, Sir Wilfrid set on his own sister, Aunt Agatha, instead. This last-named dame is a dragon who has her lair in Bath, where she breathes fire and brimstone over those ancients who play Pope Joan for pennies, wear wanton gowns that show their wrists, and on the weekend may stay up till ten o'clock. If I were Perdita, I would sooner have married Mr. Croft. Really he would have made an appropriate match for her, a stern old Puritan with a heart black as pitch. She would have had trials and tribulations fitting her station for the next twenty years of her life. I cannot think he would have lasted longer.

She elected for Aunt Agatha, however. Letters were dispatched; we were to take the family carriage from Swindon to Chippenham, where Agatha's chaise was to pick us up, thus obviating the need for either branch of the family to get into the expensive business of hiring teams. All went fine as far as Chippenham, though it was actually a thoroughly miserable trip. Perdita's little chin fairly dragged the floor, as she repined in her dramatical way about the cruelty of Fate, and her having been specially selected by God to bear these hardships.

"It seems a spiteful sort of decision to come from the Almighty. It sounds more like the work of Lady Brodie to me," I answered gruffly. It does not do to show Perdita too much sympathy when she is in this mood.

8

"If she is too harsh, I shall run away," she went on, glancing out the window.

I felt the rumblings of apprehension in my bowels, for this threat had been aired more than once since her father's marriage, and she was wilful and capricious enough to carry out the threat. "That would not accomplish much, would it?" I asked, with an air of indifference. "Where would you run to?" Her answer was of more than academic interest. In the not unlikely case that I would soon be chasing after her, it would be well to have an inkling of her destination.

"Why, to London, of course! Perdita Robinson played *A Winter's Tale* there, at the Theater Royal. It is where she landed the Prince of Wales."

"It is a great pity your mama ever named you after Mrs. Robinson," I said wearily. "I cannot imagine what she was about, giving you the nickname of an actress, and one of such shady character as well."

"They say I look like her, Papa's old friends, who saw her when she was playing Perdita on the stage."

"It is not a compliment, my dear. She was extremely plain, to judge by the pictures I have seen."

"Everyone said she was beautiful," Perdita replied, untying her bonnet and shaking out her golden curls. Gold light shone from them, bright as a new guinea. "If you say she was not as beautiful as I am, then . . ."

"I did not say so!"

"You meant it, so perhaps I could do even better than a Prince."

"With luck you might become mistress of Napoleon Bonaparte, or King Louis of France."

"Or Lord Byron," she said, in her soft, drawling way. Lord Byron was this Season's crush. The year before it had been the Duke of Wellington, and the year before that she was still more interested in her puppies and kittens. "Would it not be wonderful to be loved by a *poet,* Moira?"

9

"Marvelous, especially by one who has made himself the scandal of the country by carrying on with all the married ladies."

"Oh but to tame a rake—such a challenge! I would love to do it."

"Would he stay tamed? There is the question."

"You have no romance in your soul, Cousin. What a very dreary life you invent for yourself."

"Yes, I have contrived a remarkably dreary existence, minding *you,* but I had a little help from your nemesis, Fate. What would you expect me to contrive, with no money and no home?"

"You should have gone on the stage," she answered at once, nonplussed at my lack of wits.

"My mama forgot to christen me Perdita. That was her mistake."

"Poor Moira," she said, patting my fingers. "Never fear *I* shall desert you. When I am married, or a famous actress, you shall be my faithful companion. When my lovers abuse me, when my career falters, when I am old and not quite so beautiful and another incognita steals my place, *you* will be there to look after me. I shall have consumption, and lie on a couch."

"What a charming future to look forward to. Ah, here we are at Chippenham. I wonder which inn we were to stop at. The coachman will know. The George, I expect," I said, casting an eye over the two establishments, kitty-corner from each other. The George, as we drove closer, was seen to be the more respectable of the two. The other, the Red Lion, had a seedy, run-down appearance. There were some undesirable types littering up the street in front of it too, men in poorly-cut, brightly-colored jackets, and females in gowns that should not have been on the street in daylight.

Perdita was much interested in these inferior persons. Her practiced eye picked out what had escaped mine. "They are *actors!*" she said, standing up inside

10

the carriage in her excitement, and bumping her head against the ceiling.

I had taken the females at least for worse, but there was such a quantity of them that they could hardly *all* be lightskirts, assembled in the one place at one time. I got a firm grip on her elbow to lead her to the safety of the George, as the groom took our carriage around to the stableyard.

I was apprehensive to hear within that Aunt Agatha had not yet arrived. But upon consideration, I decided that she must be on her way, nearly here. We had left early, and set a brisk pace as Sir Wilfrid kept prime cattle. She would expect to find us in a private parlor. Anything less would set her hackles up before ever we left Chippenham. It seemed a dreadful waste of money, but Sir Wilfrid had given me twenty-five pounds, twenty-three of which were rolled up in the toe of a stocking in my trunk. I parted with some cash carried in my reticule for emergencies such as this, and hired the smallest parlor, leaving word at the desk where we were to be found when Miss Brodie, Aunt Agatha, arrived.

Before two seconds were up, Perdita had got the window raised and was sticking her head out to ogle the actors, who were having their accouterments of the stage loaded into some carriages to be on their way. The first carriage looked like a gypsy's rig. It was painted bright blue, and bore the name of the troupe in gilt letters on the side. Tuck's Traveling Theater it was called, obviously an inferior itinerant outfit that toured the counties, eking out a living by presenting bad comedy and worse singing and dancing, to amuse the farmers and villagers.

I stood behind Perdita's shoulder, where I could see without being seen, for while I disparage her interest, I am not *totally* without imagination myself. After a quarter of a century on the planet, however, I had traced the line between phantasy and reality, and stayed on the latter side. Still, I can understand what in that life would attract a young lady who has led a dull, sheltered existence, unappreciated by the world at large. It would be exciting, interesting, fun, of a low sort. With Peridita's bent for admiration, the stage had always held a lure out to her. While we both looked, with myself keeping a sharp eye for the approach of the Dragon's chaise, a monkey in a pink skirt with a bow pinned to its head joined the players. It just seemed to pop up from nowhere, but was soon being lifted on to the shoulder of a young man in the group.

He was the best looking fellow there, a fact which would surely not have escaped Perdita's eye, as it had struck even mine. "He must be the leading man," she said, speaking over her shoulder to me, her voice soft with interest. "Isn't he *handsome,* Moira?"

There was a certain self-assured swagger to his movements that attracted the attention of the females. "Not bad, in a vulgar, tawdry sort of a way," I admitted, with more attention to his wadded shoulders and nipped waist, his carefully curled locks and the monkey than to his face.

"Oh I think he's ever so handsome," she breathed, in her ecstatic voice. She had a whole range of voices, modulated to suit every occasion. She practiced them before her mirror, along with the manual and body gestures required for the stage. She had been at this for years. It gave me quite a turn three years ago when first I went to be her governess, to see her standing in a corner, wide-eyed, shouting at the top of her lungs. I thought there would be a mouse at least under the bed, but what was there was a copy of *Macbeth* on top of it, open at the sleepwalking scene. Later I learned the simulation of boisterous laughing, soft cooing sounds, tears and tantrums was all a part of her self-taught dramatic academy's curriculum. The ecstatic voice presently in use was generally reserved for falling in love.

12

I could not say whether it was herself, the leading man, or the monkey who instituted the next step in our morning. I think the man saw the girl, saw the interest on her pretty face, and put the monkey up to it. In any case, before you could say "Out, out damned spot," the monkey was hopping across the street to offer Perdita an orange, which she accepted with a smile to the monkey, and a long, calculating nod to the monkey's master. He immediately got his shoulders rolling across the street. What should happen at that moment but a black chaise came round the corner, which I naturally assumed would be Miss Brodie, catching us out in an indiscretion. I grabbed Perdita from the window, and slammed it so fast and hard it rattled the glass. The leading man's face was not visible. All we could see was the top of his blond curls, smeared with some grease. He stayed there, outside the window, for a few moments, while I explained my action to Perdita.

"He'll think we are awfully rude," she said, beginning to peel the orange.

"Put that down, you fool! It has been handled by a monkey. You'll get hydrophobia."

"I'm hungry," she said, forgetting to use her abused child's voice.

"There is no time to eat now. You aunt is here. I'll go to the desk and remind them to send her in to us."

Who dismounted from the carriage was not Miss Brodie, but a country vicar and his family, half a dozen noisy children. I ordered tea, to help us pass our wait. When I returned to the parlor, I was treated to a fine view of Perdita's derrière. Her head and shoulders were out the window. She was flirting as hard as she could with the leading man. I pulled her in, using both hands to do it. "I hope you and your monkey will excuse us. We are busy. Good day," I said to the suitor, then closed the window and slid the lock on top if it.

"He's Irish," was her comment when I turned a

13

wrathful stare on her. "The Irish have lovely eyes, don't you think?"

"I never noticed."

"*I* am Irish, too—of Irish ancestry I mean. His name is Daugherty. He has such a sweet brogue. 'Sure an' your eyes are like a little bit of heaven,' he said to me." She had a pretty good imitation of the brogue already picked up.

"That sounds a nice civil introduction. I have ordered tea. It wasn't Miss Brodie's carriage after all."

She kept glancing towards the window. With it firmly closed and locked, I saw no harm to let her look, but requested her to stay behind the curtains at least. We both watched the antics of the actors till the tea tray arrived, our prime interest being to select the leading lady from the half dozen females who were making eyes at Mr. Daugherty. Perdita thought the fulsome redhead in broad green and yellow stripes was the one, but as this female was obviously over thirty, I picked out a pretty little blonde instead.

We were both wrong. In a few minutes, a queenly creature strutted forth from the inn door. She wore a great plate of a bonnet, with three curling ostrich plumes trailing behind. She also wore a fur cape, despite the warm breezes of spring. She carried a pug dog in her arms, and was accompanied by a dragon not unlike Miss Brodie. The group fell back to let her pass. The first carriage, the one with Tuck's Traveling Theater printed on the side, was her chariot. A young urchin threw open the door, and she entered. Mr. Daugherty, with a last look over his shoulder towards our window, went and joined her in the carriage. The team were given the office, and they were off in a cloud of dust.

A wistful sigh escaped Perdita's lips, as she gazed forlornly out the window at them "They are on their way to London," she said, "with stops at

14

Marlborough, Kingsclere, Farnborough and possibly Woking, if the theater manager there does not welch on his bargain. They play what is called in the theater 'one night stands,' Moira. Next year they will tour larger cities, and eventually they hope to play the Lane or the Garden. That is what theater people call Drury Lane and Covent Garden," she informed me, having become an instant expert in matters dramatical.

"Mr. Daugherty gave you a quick lesson, did he?"

"Yes, he was very nice. He thinks I am a great dramatic tragedian, for I told him I am not at all interested in mere comedy. Tuck's Players are comedians," she added, in a condescending way.

I heard more of the wisdom of Mr. Daugherty over tea. I cannot believe he had time to tell her half the things she told me. It was nearly noon by the time tea was done, and still Aunt Agatha had not arrived. I went to the desk to inquire once more, beginning to feel like a pest. A note was handed to me, just arrived, the clerk said, though it was sitting under a bell, which suggested it had been there long enough to have found a home. I tore it open eagerly, to read the dreadful news that Miss Brodie was abed with a bad case of influenza, which she thought it unwise to transmit to us. She had just that morning had her doctor confirm the diagnosis, and he suggested we go home, and postpone our visit for a week.

I took the sorrowful news back to Perdita. Her bottom lip began quivering, while a great, crystal-clear tear—really a diamond of a tear—welled up in her eyes, to tremble a moment on the brink, before oozing down her cheek. "They will make me marry Mr. Croft," she said in pitiful accents.

"Indeed they will not. They will let us go to Aunt Maude, as we wanted to in the first place. Brighton will be much gayer than Bath. You'll see."

"No, they won't. I *begged* Papa to let me go to Brighton, but he said it would be full of rakes and

15

rattles, and I would fall into mischief. Oh, Moira, what am I to do? Mr. Croft will come around again, preaching of piety and pretending to Papa he is so holy, when I know in my bones he is *horrid*. It is all Lady Brodie's doings, shuffling me out of the house, because she hates me."

"You must do what your father says, Perdita. It will be all right. We'll go to Bath next week. One week won't make much difference."

"I am not going back," she said sullenly. "Let us go to Brighton. This is our chance. Mama's sister will be able to talk Papa around to letting us stay, once we are there. He really admires Aunt Maude, you know. It is only that he does not want me to go and tell her how horrid his new wife is. That is why he won't let me go, but once I have gone and told her, then there will be no point in making me come back."

"Let me think a moment," I said, sinking on to a chair. I really felt extremely sorry for her, and apprehensive for her future. Her father had been quite set on the match with Croft. To return might well precipitate a hasty wedding, for while Croft was in the boughs at the moment, he was still interested. Aunt Maude was the best of our relatives, my own cousin as well as Perdita's aunt. My charge and I are related on the maternal side, which is how I came to be her governess when Mama died. Besides being nice, Maude is quite a strong character. She would give Sir Wilfrid a hard time, if she knew what was afoot. I had written her a letter informing her of Sir Wilfrid's plans, but she never replied. I could not know whether she had been away on some holiday when it arrived, or whether, as I suspected later, the letter was never posted. I had left it with Sir Wilfrid's mail in the silver mail salver at home. I could not like to barge in at Brighton if she were away, or unwell. What would we do if she were not there? No, it would be better to stay where we were till we had

16

time to write again and ask Maude if we might come. There would be no trouble at home, in Swindon. They would think we were safely at Bath; for a few days or a week we could con them we were there, as it was not likely Aunt Agatha would rise up from her sickbed to write Sir Wilfrid.

I outlined my plan to Perdita. She was inordinately pleased. "You must not put too much hope in it, my dear," I told her. "It is not certain Aunt Maude will be in a position to have us."

"If she cannot, I'll go to Alton's," she answered, undaunted. "John is in London for the Season. I can stay with him and his mother."

"Your papa will not like your putting up with a bachelor, even if he is a neighbor."

"His mother is there. Papa is only afraid I might marry him, but I never would. He is not at all romantic."

John Alton was not rich or socially high enough to be eligible for Perdita, whereas Mr. Croft owned an abbey. "What I would do is find some other handsome gentleman to marry. So long as he was rich and preferably noble, Papa would not care in the least."

"True, but that can be done from Brighton. We'll try Aunt Maude first."

"Promise me you won't make me go back," she pleaded.

"I shall do what I can. I can't *promise*. If your Aunt Maude cannot have us at this time, we must go home, but I shall help you escape Mr. Croft. I promise you that."

She looked at me, a half-disappointed, disillusioned look, but in the end had no choice but to accept it. I wrote to Maude, and Perdita left the letter off at the desk while I arranged for our trunks to be unloaded. The carriage must be sent home, to make Sir Wilfrid think we had made contact with Aunt Agatha, as arranged. We had to hire a sleeping room, as we

17

would be staying for a night or two. Our trunks were taken above, and for the remainder of the day we enjoyed a holiday, walking around the town, looking through the shops, and discussing at length what form our future was likely to take. I could not like to worry her, but if Aunt Maude was not agreeable to have us, I would certainly be turned off from my post for having abetted Perdita in this scheme. It was not a detail to sit lightly on my heart. How should I help her, in that case?

Before dinner, I tired of walking and went to our room to go through my address book, canvassing other possible havens for us, if things turned out for the worst. Perdita became bored, and went belowstairs to get some newspapers. Later, we had dinner in our room, which looked out on the main street of the little town.

"There is one of those carriages from Tuck's, still at the Red Lion," I mentioned.

"There is to be no play tonight," she told me. "Mr. Daugherty was going ahead to arrange the business and finances at Marlborough, then the others are to join him tomorrow, and put on their play at night. Do you suppose the woman in the ostrich feathers was his wife, Moira? He did not say he was married."

"I have no idea. Is Daugherty not an actor after all, then?"

"Oh yes, the leading actor, also the manager, and he writes their stuff too, like Shakespeare. I wonder what the Tuck stands for. You would think he would call it the Daugherty Players."

"I am surprised he does not call it the King's Men."

"He was not allowed. They made him change it last year when he went to London. Shall we go for a walk before we turn in for the night? It will be a long, dull evening in our room."

"We cannot go on the streets unescorted. It is nearly dark."

"The actresses are having a stroll."

"Precisely!"

Instead of walking, we went to the window and observed the passing parade. It provided an excellent hour's entertainment. I had not seen so interesting a spectacle since first clapping my eyes on the new Lady Brodie. The girls were not walking, but making up to any male pedestrian who passed by. As often as not, the man in question would enter the Red Lion with the actress. Before our show was called off because of darkness, I believe every one of the girls had picked up an escort in this highly irregular fashion. We had some difficulty in sleeping for the racket coming to us from across the road, where the windows were open, with singing, shouting, and the hammering of an out-of-tune piano blaring into the night.

Chapter Two

I awoke in the morning to the unusual sight of King George III in his parliamentary robes, glaring at me from the foot of the bed. He was in a frame, of course, hanging from the wall. By his side hung a hideous green parrot, done in clothwork. I was trying to decide which was the uglier when I became aware of something unusual. Glancing across at the pillow beside me, I saw it was empty. The imprint of Perdita's head was on it still, but the girl was gone. No terror consumed my being. I knew she was not a late sleeper. She was up and dressed, probably in the dining room below having her breakfast. A look at my watch told me it was after eight, time that I arise and join her.

I rang for warm water, made a leisurely toilette, as there was really nothing to do all day long but wait. We could not expect to hear from Maude before the next day. My hope was that she would come in person to collect us. A half hour had elapsed before I entered the dining hall. Still no panic surged when Perdita was not there. She had finished and gone for a walk, before the town was bustling with activity. I had toast and tea, and stopped at the desk to see if the newspapers had arrived yet. The clerk, the same I had seen badgering for word of Aunt Agatha the day before, was on duty.

"This time I have your message waiting for you, ma'am," he said, handing me a white folded paper.

"Thank you," I replied, wondering who it could be from. Mr. Daugherty popped into my head. Before I read a word, I recognized Perdita's peculiar penmanship. Her somewhat childishly-formed letters were always ornamented with swirls and curlicues, while her i's were dotted with v's. And still, fool that I am, I thought only how considerate she was to have left me word in what direction she was walking, in case I wished to join her.

It was nothing of the sort. She started right off her epistle with a melodramatic outburst of how she could not *endure* this cruel life that was before her, and to free her soul of the fetters of constraint, she was fleeing 'while still Time Remayned.' Spelling was never her forte. Any word that was not given a capital was underlined to add force to her persuasions. No destination was named, but it hardly took a wizard to conclude she had run to Tuck's Traveling Theater. I darted out the door to see if the carriage were still standing by. The roadway was empty.

I had to screw up my courage to enter the disreputable Red Lion alone to inquire when they had left. "The actors went last night, miss," the proprietor told me. "It's their custom to leave at night. In that way they can sleep in their carriages, and save a night's lodging. Their regular way of carrying on," he added in a disparaging, gypped tone.

"But they were here late last night. I heard them."

"Aye, so did the whole town. They stayed drinking and hollering till past midnight, but they didn't sleep over. I'm not sorry to see the backs of them."

I asked, pink with shame, if a young lady had joined them, but he had no knowledge of my charge.

22

While I had the ear of a local, I asked for the hours of the coach, only to learn I had missed one by fifteen minutes. Another would not be past till noon. He was kind enough to direct me to a hostelry that rented carriages.

I darted back to the George first to get my money, and have our trunks brought down for loading on a hired carriage. That was when the day's second calamity struck. I was painfully aware too that mishaps generally occur in three's. The maid had been in our room and made it up. I went rooting through the trunk for the precious stocking holding our money, to find our things had been thoroughly rifled. The money was gone, likewise a few small items of wearing apparel. I needed that money too desperately to do without it.

I stormed down to the desk, demanded the manager, made a great thundering brouhaha. Maids were called into his office, a search of their persons and rooms carried out, the whole of it using up a great deal of precious time and patience.

"Nothing for it, ma'am, we'll have to call in a constable," the manager said apologetically.

"I am in a great hurry. Could you not forward me some money? I don't need the whole twenty-three pounds. Five or ten will do."

The fisheye he raked me with was a revelation. He did not believe a word of my story. Suggesting less than the whole sum convinced him I was shamming it. "Afraid that is impossible. Go to the constable—if you dare," he said, with a brazen look.

Before I left, he added one dim ray of hope. "Maybe your cohort took the blunt with her when she ran," he said, in an odiously offending manner.

I hoped and prayed she had, but could not believe it. Perdita had not bothered to take her own things; why would she have taken my tippet with the mink tails, or my best lace collar, which items were also missing?

23

My next stop was the hiring stable. Having left it so late, there was nothing to be had but a whiskey. It hardly mattered. I could not have afforded a regular carriage, team and groom in any case. In fact, I had to leave my obligation at the inn unfulfilled, as I had less than two pounds to see Perdita and myself to safety. Our trunks were left behind as hostages. I would go after Perdita, come back to the George and sit tight till Maude got in touch with us. If she did not come in person, we were sunk.

The nag they hitched up to the whiskey was as old as Adam. Dawdle is too racy a word for her gait. I could have walked on my own two feet faster, though not so far. The old jade, Ginger she was named, hinting at a livelier youth, poked along at a frisky two or so miles an hour, till at last a road marker loomed ahead, at a crossroads. I was alert for the markers as the territory was not familiar to me, but I remembered Marlborough had been named by Perdita as the troupe's next stop. The word Marlborough did not appear. Devizes, five miles, the marker said.

Fearful that I was on the wrong road, I stopped at the next farm for direction. Yes, the farmer's wife told me, I would have made better time had I turned left a mile back, but there was no sign posted, as she recalled, for everyone knew well enough the route to Marlborough. I was not more than a mile or two out of my way, if I just cared to turn Ginger around and head back. There was a tantalizing aroma of freshly-baked bread on the air, the sizzle of bacon coming from her kitchen, and a hole as big as a boot inside of me, for the day was wearing on. A feeble question as to the closest inn where I could take luncheon brought forth the hoped-for offer.

"Have you not ate yet?" she asked, astonished. "Why, miss, it's two o'clock. I've fed the hands an hour ago, and am just making up a mess of beans

24

and bacon for myself. Join me, do. I don't get much company."

I bolted the meal with unseemly haste, outlining as I ate that I was in a dreadful hurry, but changing some of the details to protect the guilty party. I implied I was on my way to a deathbed, which satisfied the woman as to my incoherent condition. Ginger did not increase her pace as the afternoon dragged on. Quite the contrary. I was strongly tempted to jump out and push her up the hills, of which there are an inordinate number, all of them going up, on the road from Chippenham to Marlborough. There was ample time to worry myself sick, to plan lectures for Perdita, to pity her, to wonder if I had done the right thing in not taking her home, to know I had not, yet to confirm that almost any fate was better than Mr. Croft. The sun became hot as the afternoon wore on, but when I put off my pelisse, the wind was chilly. All in all, it was about the least enjoyable drive I have ever endured.

There was some doubt too, towards its end, as to whether Ginger was going to go the course. A dead horse to cope with seemed an appropriate third calamity to visit me. When we approached the harbingers of Marlborough, Ginger was still hacking. The houses grew closer together, signs of commercial establishements sprang up—bakery, abattoir, tannery. The sun had not quite set when at last I pushed Ginger into town.

I decided to stable her at once, leave her off at the hostelry agreed upon in Chippenham, before she dropped from exhaustion. With this done, my next project was to discover my charge, before she mounted a stage, to discredit her fair reputation forever. Tuck's Traveling Theater had their handbills posted along the main street, proclaiming Reimer's Hall as the scene of the night's performance. Unsure whether they had booked into an inn or planned to sleep in their caravan, I asked for the location of the hall, knowing they must show up there sooner or later, but certainly sooner than seven-thirty, the hour the show was to begin. The place was at the edge of town.

It was six-thirty when I reached it. It was not so large as to have any noble clients or anything of that sort. There would be no one to see her, if by any chance she had sweet-talked Daugherty into letting her take to the boards. I sound like a very ineffectual person to confess that, after coming so far, I was unable to gain entry into the hall, but so it was. The front door was locked, the back door was locked. I banged and hammered at both entrances, without getting an answer. The windows were too high off the ground to effect an entry in daylight. Had it been dark, I would have tried it.

I was so tired and so frustrated that in the end I decided to have some dinner, and go like a patron to the hall a quarter of an hour before the performance began. Dinner was only nominally dinner. A lone lady did not venture into a common room. I had a sandwich at a teashop, the last customer to enter, just before the door was locked. Anger was rising to the top of my emotions as I paid my way into Reimer's Hall, reducing my cash to practically nothing. Once inside I did not take a seat, but went backstage, ready to pull Perdita by the scruff of the neck out of the disreputable place.

I blush to relate the conditions under which the troupe made their preparations. The females were wedged, three or four to a cubicle, behind hanging curtains that did not even come to the floor. There were ten or twelve inches of ankle and leg exposed. The women darted in and out with no great regard for pulling the curtain closed behind them. The place was a voyeur's delight. There were several greasy-looking men just outside, peering greedily in each time the curtain was opened. Being a stranger in their midst, I was subjected to my share of scru-

26

tiny from the bucks. When one of them rolled up to me, with his great wadded shoulders sticking out a foot from his body, I asked in the haughtiest tone I own for Mr. Daugherty.

The man looked me boldly up and down, hunched his wadding as though to imply my anatomy was not up to the company's high standard, then walked away, waving a hand for me to follow in his footsteps.

Mr. Daugherty had set aside a cubbyhole for himself amidst the backstage squalor. I think it was a broom closet actually. In it he sat with a wine bottle and a glass, bent over a sheet of closely-written figures, balanced on his knee. He did not recognize me.

After repeating the ocular examination that was apparently an inevitable result of a female's venturing behind stage, he asked "What's your act, miss? I have all the girls I can use, unless you have something special to offer."

"I am not looking for work, sir. I am looking for my charge, who joined you at Chippenham last night."

He raised his brows, hunched his shoulders, threw out his hands and regarded me with a conning smile. "I don't know what you're talking about, miss. I was in Marlborough last night," he said, with an Irish accent that I shan't attempt to duplicate. It added something to his speech, but would detract from the telling to go jumbling up the letters.

"Your outfit was in Chippenham. She joined it," I said coolly, though I did not actually *know* anything of the sort. "If you do not produce her this instant, I shall call in a constable. She is a minor, under my charge."

"A minor, you say?"

"That's right. Any attempt to force her . . ."

"Force! Nay, you've got the wrong end of the stick I swear. There was no *forcing*," he said at once, an expression of alarmed fear lighting on his visage, which was rather handsome, incidentally.

"When it is a *minor* in question, the onus falls on the older party," I said, not sure of my legal facts, but sure Mr. Daugherty would have no notion whether they were true, nor question them, so long as they sounded bold and menacing.

He licked his lips, ran his fingers nervously through his hair, and blurted out the truth. "She's gone to sit in the audience and see the show."

As I turned to leave, he called after me, "But I didn't *force* her. She came running after us!"

I knew perfectly well it was true, so said nothing, but only hurried out to scan the audience for her bold face. What an audience it was! The worst rabble ever assembled in the country, ninety percent of it male, and the other ten percent lightskirts. I felt perfectly degraded to enter the hall, but at least Perdita was sitting in a dark corner with an elderly, decent-looking woman to guard her. She tried to slink down behind the woman when she spotted me, but she knew it was futile, and finally sat up and waved instead.

Chapter Three

The show had not yet begun. I slid onto the chair beside her and got a hard hold of her arm. "Get your pelisse. We are leaving this hole, at once."

"Must we?" she asked. "Can't we stay and see the performance at least? It is just about to begin."

Between a desire to see it, fatigue, the lack of anywhere to go when we left and plain dereliction of duty, I allowed myself to be talked into remaining for a while, which of course turned into the whole performance. The production owed everything but its title to John Gay's *Beggar's Opera*. It was so close a copy of the work that Mr. Daugherty ought to have been imprisoned as a plagiarist for daring to attach his name to it as author, and changing the title to *The Warder's Daughter*. Mr. Daugherty played Captain Macheath, under the title of Colonel Maciver. Our leading lady of the ostrich plumes played Lucy, and a rather pretty blonde was Polly. It was an extremely entertaining performance. I doubt there was a troupe in London who could have done better. Mr. Daugherty looked very handsome in his officer's uniform, sporting every manner of ribbon and medal.

The rivals for his affection put on an excellent cat fight, while the fellow who played the fence was masterful, a walking weasel. We were fairly well concealed in our dark corner, so that we suffered no stares or rudeness from the male audience.

It was no polite play that was put on. The ribaldry was so high at times I had to blush, and try to distract Perdita's attention. Maciver took such freedoms with the women onstage I actually feared the police would come in and arrest him for putting on an obscene performance. When the two girls were fighting, too, it was arranged so that their dresses were half over their heads, and half down to their waists. Really quite shocking, but all done in a spirit of fun, offending no one but myself, and I was only offended from a sense of duty.

When the curtain came down at intermission, I took the opportunity to quiz Perdita as to what she had been doing all day. She had skipped out of the George the night before as soon as she heard me snore. I do not *snore* actually, but groan in my sleep sometimes when I am troubled. She nipped over to the Red Lion and joined Tuck's outfit. She had got a letter from Daugherty in her pocket, left off at the inn before his departure, inviting her. It is *almost* incredible she had accomplished so much during a brief talk at a window, but I have learned to believe the incredible from her. When she showed them the letter, she was taken aboard with no trouble.

"He has a deal of gall, asking you to join him!"

"I told him I was an actress," she confessed. "But a very high class tragic actress."

"Fool! What was the point asking you to join this farcical play then?"

"He said he would write a great tragedy for me. Something like *Macbeth,* as I already know the lines."

"Yes, and call it Macheath, as he changed Gay's character's name."

"Meanwhile he said I could sing or dance. They have songs after the ballad opera. He is very nice, and he is *not* married to Phoebe either, though she is jealous as a green cow of him. Phoebe is the leading lady."

"I don't suppose you happened to take our money when you left the inn?"

"Good gracious no! I could not leave you stranded and penniless! I forgot all about the money," she added, to defeat her claim. "I expect we will have to stay overnight at Marlborough, and hire a carriage back to Chippenham tomorrow to await Aunt Maude."

"The money is gone. Stolen from the inn, every sou of it. I have two shillings to my name. Do you think Daugherty might lend us a few pounds?"

"They are very short of funds. He says the play made Gay rich, and Daugherty poor. I don't know what it means, but they are going to sleep overnight in their carriages. They aren't even dormeuses, but they have got pillows and things to make quite a comfortable bed. I'm sure he would let you stay too, if you like," she offered.

"How exceedingly kind of him!" I answered ironically, but in fact this low means of spending the night was something of a relief, the alternative being the open road or the almshouse.

Perdita did not reply, nor even hear me. Her eyes had strayed off to the side of the hall, where some new arrivals were making a grand and noisy entrance. It was only two people, two gentlemen, but they managed to make such a to do that every head in the place turned to stare at them, including my own. One would think they set out to claim as much notice as possible. They were outfitted in a manner at odds with every other man in the place. They wore fashionable black evening clothes, a triangle of pristine white shirt-front highly visible across the hall. They talked and laughed noisily, not noticing or caring that everyone was observing them. They were not observing much of anything, I think, for they appeared to have taken on a deal of wine. Their barbering, their general get-up and behavior did not speak of the provinces. This pair had come from London, to go slumming in the countryside. They were, unfortunately, both young and handsome.

One was dark and heavy-set, with broad shoulders but a trim waist. The other was taller, more aristocratic-looking somehow, with a thin, chiselled face and a slighter build. Before we had more time to observe them, the curtain opened and Lucy came rushing on to the stage, in a pucker because Macivor had been thrown into gaol. She looked wantonly attractive, in a low-cut white blouse, topped off with a tight-fitting weskit that was pulled in to display her tiny waist, which was made to appear even smaller by the generous swell of bosoms and hips on top and bottom. The city visitors actually let out whistles and howls of appreciation. Their vociferous praise incited the other men in the hall to emulate them. The rest of the play was pure farce. There were catcalls, foot stompings, shouts, whistles, and at the end a shower of coins rained on the stage. I wished I could dart up, collect them, and flee this den of lechery. The newcomers had removed the last vestige of decency from the evening. I knew I was attending an orgy.

"Perdita, we must leave now," I said. I could not trust the smiles she was throwing to the two bucks. Our only salvation was that they never once removed their eyes from the stage. "Let us go to that carriage you mentioned and make ourselves comfortable."

"I had better check with Mr. Daugherty first," she replied.

This sounded reasonable, but I had no thought of letting her go alone. "They don't like strangers backstage during the performance," she said.

The older woman who had been sitting with her

was the group's seamstress, who had earlier explained grandly that she was "the wardrobe mistress." A spade would doubtlessly be termed "an earth-turning utensil" by Tuck's troupe. "I'll go with her," she volunteered. "I have to get the costumes and check them out for rips. That Phoebe has her gowns so tight she splits a seam every performance."

I sunk lower in my seat, disliking to be alone, but I must say no one paid any heed to me. I remained totally unmolested. The other females in the audience were much more interesting. The city bucks had removed across the aisle to set up a flirtation with two local belles, who were much inclined to honor their attentions. The delay between the ballad opera and the songs was longer than seemed necessary. The reason for it was to allow the hawkers to sell their wares. The Tom and Jerry from London bought an entire basket of oranges and nuts, and proceeded to make a great display of tossing them round to the audience.

At last, Mr. Daugherty came through the curtain to announce the songs and singers. My sense of disaster had improved since leaving the inn. I had a premonition, when he started puffing off a new girl, that my third calamity had come, with a vengeance. The new girl was Perdita. The only saving grace was that he had the wits to call her by another name. In honour of the season, he called her Miss April Spring. Really!

She was got up in an outfit that was surely designed for wear in a bordello. It consisted of about two yards of transparent red gauze, sprinkled strategically with white flowers. There was a lamp shining behind her, lest any hard-of-seeing gentleman be deprived of her outline. Her blond hair had been stirred up with a spoon, to sit in beguiling disorder above her painted face. She carried a large fan of white ostrich feathers, which I wished she would hold in front of her body to hide her shame, but she did not. She perched it over her left shoulder, as she began to sing a travesty of a ballad. "Woeful Heart with Grief Oppressed" was her first rendition. It was perfectly *wretched*. The private dramatic academy had not taught song, only overacting. Her voice was small, high, light and off-key. She was nervous too, which added an air of discomfort to the performance. I hardly knew whether to laugh, cry or hang my head in shame. But as I considered, I thought it might be a good lesson for her if the audience gave her a sound boohing.

Hah! Boohing indeed! They *loved* her. It was not the voice that was under inspection, but the body. The applause at the song's end would deafen an auctioneer. It was led by the city bucks, who stood up to give her a standing ovation, while they urged, nay—commanded, the others to do likewise, meanwhile bellowing "More! More!," as if their lives depended on it. She did not disappoint them. After a hurried and amateurish discussion with the man who beat the piano, she informed her fans she would sing for them "Deare, if You Change," followed by "Faire, Sweet, Cruel." The singing did not improve but got noticeably worse as her voice creaked; then at one point broke under the strain of singing louder and longer than she was used to. She became emboldened as she went along. She began mincing about the stage, batting her fan at the audience, playing with them, rolling her eyes, tossing her head, doing everything but lift her skirts to show them her knees.

It was too much provocation for the city bucks. They could not retain their seats. They edged closer and closer to the stage, creeping down the aisle, till at the last verse of "Faire, Sweet, Cruel" they had their elbows leaning on it. As she made her final bow, the taller of the two bounded up on the stage and followed her off, while the audience roared their appreciation of this piece of lechery.

I waited no longer, but bolted out to find my way backstage. I wasn't a minute too soon. He already had his arms around her, trying to pull her head into line for an attack. I thought she would be frightened, weeping, hysterical. There were rather wild sounds issuing from her lips, but as I got closer, I saw she was laughing, and saw as well that the lecher was tickling her. He was not such a young man, either. I doubt he was a day under thirty, but of course he was as drunk as a wheelbarrow. His face was flushed, his voice slurred, his legs unsteady, his manner positively insulting.

"My little pocket Venus!" he crooned, as he tried to focus his rolling eyes on her face.

"Come, at once!" I decreed, pulling her hand and trying to disengage her.

"Not poaching, ma'am," he assured me, with a foolish smile. "Want to buy her fair and square. Name your price."

I lifted my reticule and swotted the side of his head, causing him to fall back against the wall, where he shook himself to rights, trying to stand up straight. His condition made it impossible for him to follow when I pulled Perdita off into a room and slammed the door. I leaned my full weight against it, then lit into her, castigating her as everything from a fool to a lightskirt, with the morals of an alley cat. She smiled serenely, and informed me I was jealous, as she preened her mop of tangles with her fingers, and shook out her fan.

At length, Daugherty came, knocked, announced himself, and was allowed to enter.

"His friend has taken him away," he said apologetically. "We are bothered by these city fellows as we get close to London. They come out to look over the girls, you know, and make nuisances of themselves."

"Just what are you running here, Mr. Daugherty, a theatrical group or a ring of prostitution?" I demanded angrily. I had never uttered such words before, but from having been associated with the army in my youth, I had learned them at a young age.

"I don't encourage the fellows. They walk off with my prettiest wenches. Honey attracts flies, ma'am. Always has, always will. The honey is happy enough to find a profitable comb, if it comes to that."

"And what got into *you* to climb up on that stage and make a scandal of yourself?" I asked, turning to vent my fury on Perdita. I spoke more sharply, knowing it was nine-tenths my own fault. I had made it possible, when my job was to prevent it.

"You said you wanted to stay overnight. *Naturally* we must pay our way. Everyone in the group has to. Daugherty does not allow any freeloaders, and we don't have any money. It was very kind of him to let me work it off," she said, with a smirk that was intended for a smile in his direction.

"You have turned into a wanton in the space of twenty-four hours!"

"This one is a natural-born performer," Daugherty told me, in that pious manner of one explaining the Lord's will to a nonbeliever. "It is best for you to slip her out to the carriage before the fellow sobers up and starts looking for her. He fell asleep in a corner. He is in no position to close tonight." I did not understand his last sentence, but took it for a piece of theater jargon.

"Will we be safe?"

"Certainly you will. They won't know you are there. How should they?"

"Why I thought perhaps you used the carriages as dens of vice, when you were not traveling!" I answered sharply.

I spoke in angry jest, but the conscious look that descended on his face hinted I had hit upon the truth. "I won't let anyone near you," he promised. "You can have the blue dormeuse to yourselves.

Phoebe will have my hair out by the roots, but I'll palm her off with some story."

"Come along, then," I said, taking Perdita by the hand.

"My clothes!" she reminded me. I had not the courage to ask where she had changed them.

Daugherty was obliging enough to go for her gown, and hand it to us, while the monkey was given her petticoat to carry. The monkey too earned its keep. It had some small part in the night's farce. He was doing his best for us, and really it was not Daugherty's fault we had fallen into such a nasty pickle, so before leaving, I thanked him very civilly. I could not but wonder, as we entered to make our preparations for bed in a carriage, why he was being so kind. The unhappy thought would intrude that he hoped to have my charge appear again onstage, as she had been such a resounding success. We might count ourselves fortunate if he did not blazon her name and likeness on the broadbills handed out in the village before a performance.

It was dark in the carriage, but the pulling out of the seats to make a bed had already been taken care of. Decadent satin pillows and sheets awaited Phoebe's pleasure. I had an uneasy inkling we were doing Daugherty as well out of a bed for the night. There was a smell of Macassar hair oil on my pillow that I could not explain otherwise. I did not complain of it to Perdita; she had had enough of licentiousness for one night. We shucked off our gowns, folded them as carefully as possible to lessen the wrinkles, and climbed into the uncomfortable, lumpy bed. Sleep, despite my fatigue, was the farthest thing from my mind. I had my reticule ready to fight off the advance of any rake who stuck his head in at the door, fully expecting it would happen.

I badgered Perdita for a while about her outrageous behavior, but could not give her the raking down she deserved, as it was coming to seem I must

37

allow her to repeat the songs, if we were to have even this minimal comfort tomorrow night. There was no money to return to Chippenham. I could hardly show my face at the inn either, after having left my bill unpaid. Must we wear the clothes on our backs till we could contact Aunt Maude?

"The Altons are in London *for sure,* are they, Perdita?" I asked.

"Yes, it might be best if we go that far with Mr. Daugherty, then contact them. They will take us to Maude. What do *you* think?"

"I think it is an abominable plan, but I cannot think of a better one. I wish we had gone back home."

"Well I do not! I never had such fun in my life. Did you hear the applause?"

"I am not quite deaf. I heard it. I heard that drunken libertine try to buy you too. My God, why did you not beat him?"

"I thought he was rather sweet. Phoebe was jealous as a cat. She thought he was planning to have her."

"Have her what?"

"You know."

"Yes, *I* know, and I should like to discover how *you* know."

"We had some very interesting talks in the carriage yesterday."

"Pray do not feel obliged to repeat them for my edification."

"Angie says every girl in the group hopes to find a patron when they get to London. Imagine, and *I* found one the first night."

"You did not find a patron, miss. You had the poor luck to attract the attention of a drunken rake, who planned to have his way with you. You may be thankful I got here in time."

"I wonder who he is. Phoebe will be sure to find out. She will meet him in the Green Room. There really is no Green Room at Reimer's Hall, but Angie says wherever they have their party after the show is called the Green Room, like at the Lane or the Garden. Angie is the pretty blonde who plays Polly. I told her you thought at Chippenham *she* was the leading lady. She was so pleased. She is very nice. She hates Phoebe."

"She sounds charming."

The performance in the hall finished at that point. Other singers had followed April Spring. There was suddenly a great commotion as the audience came out, but our carriage was parked at the side of the hall, so that we were a little out of the way of the traffic. We gave up trying to sleep, and peeped out from behind the curtains. The dormeuse had curtains that were drawn across for the night.

"I don't see him," Perdita said, referring to her would-be purchaser.

"Good. I hope Phoebe attaches him."

Still I was uneasy till I saw him and his friend leave. I kept taking an occasional look out the window. There was enough merriment and carousing from the Green Room within that sleep was impossible in any case. Half an hour elapsed in this tiring fashion before the two black jackets and white triangles were seen coming out the door. They did not leave at once, but stood, looking around, finally sauntering towards the trail of carriages, of which we made up a part.

"Where the hell could she have gotten to?" the pursuer asked, in vexed accents. His speech was clearer than before. Time or the fresh air was working on his condition.

"Somebody beat you to her, Storn," his friend roasted him.

"I'll cut out his heart and make him eat it. God, did you ever see such a piece of woman? Grrr." He made some low, animal sound in his throat, difficult to put into letters, but its essence was pure lust.

"'Tis pity she's a whore," his friend answered.

"*Au contraire*. A whore, a whore, my kingdom for a whore! Tell me now, was I dead drunk, or was she something out of the ordinary?"

"Get into bed, Perdita," I urged, shoving her down.

"Top of the trees," his friend agreed.

"Built like a . . . and the *bosoms,* like two ripe melons."

"Get into bed and cover your ears!" I said, trying to draw a satin sheet up over her head.

"Just a minute. They are talking about *me,*" she said, hopping back up.

"No, they are obviously talking about Phoebe."

"Not much of a voice," the darker, heavier man said.

"Voice? Did she have a voice? I didn't notice. That Venus is going to be in my pocket before she gets to London."

"Don't open that curtain!" I shrieked, but in a low voice, twitching it back into place. Perdita tittered, but contented herself to lay her ear against the window inside the curtain.

"I could learn to love that wench," the first admirer said rather wistfully. "I may not offer for Dulcinea after all." He was already practically engaged to some lady, you see, and talking so broad about Perdita.

The dark man laughed. "By God, you better keep the girl under close wraps then. Where will you take her?"

"To Birdland. Where else would I take a bird of such rare plumage? You don't suppose that damned harpy with her would expect to accompany us?"

The damned harpy felt an angry thudding in her breast.

"You can buy her off. Mind you'll have to come down heavy. You know how these abbesses are when they get a young chick like April."

"She's worth it. This is the one, Staff. This is the

40

one I've been waiting for. Who would have thought I'd flush her out of cover in Marlborough? *Marlborough,* imagine! Nowhere."

"How will you get hold of her?"

"Through Daugherty, maybe. Maybe the bawd. We shall have to see who owns her."

"Nobody owns me!" Perdita said, shocked at last.

"These men are dangerous," I cautioned.

"Old Phoebe was pretty well stuffed, too," the darker man said in an approving way.

"Bursting at the seams, but she's a bit of a tough old hen for me. I like 'em young." There was a longish silence, then he spoke again. "God, I'm drunk," he said, in a wearied voice. "Good party though. Mama will give me hell for leaving so early. We better get back to Stornaway. Twenty miles—it'll take over an hour."

"Back to Dull-cinea," the other man said, laughing.

"Dull, dull, *dull,* Dulcinea! But she's a good girl," he added, in a dutiful way.

"Top of the trees," his friend agreed readily, consigning to the lady the same epithet given Perdita.

They straggled off together, beginning to sing "Faire, Sweet, Cruel" in a very creditable duet. I was weak with relief that they had not discovered us.

"He certainly likes me," was Perdita's contented comment.

"Aren't you flattered? He wouldn't recognize you if he fell over you tomorrow. He was dead drunk."

"Oh he was not quite down among the dead men. It means out stone cold," she told me. A new piece of distinction picked up from Angie. "Anyway, it's all right. I would recognize him," she said, yawning. "His friend called him Storn, and he mentioned Stornaway. It is only twenty miles away. Someone must know who he is. The other was called Staff—it must be a nickname. Maybe he would like *you,* Moira."

"You are really too kind. Anyone who liked Phoebe

would not care for an abbess. I suppose he called me that becuase I wore a dark gown."

"Oh no, it is what gentlemen call a female who handles prostitutes," she said, in the sweetest, most innocent voice ever heard. "Angie told me. She used to work for the Abbess Rose in London, but the woman beat her and took all the money for herself, so she ran away. Poor Angie has had a hard life."

"Yes, I come to realize life on the streets without any money is not easy."

Another yawn was my reply. I set my head on the pillow, and to my utter amazement, I slept.

Chapter Four

Daylight showed me the bower in which I had so innocently slept was done up in red satin. Sheets, pillows, curtains and all were blood-red satin. The sun filtering through the windows bathed the whole in a fiery glow, turning us into a pair of scarlet women. Perdita still slept. I made as little disturbance as possible struggling into my gown. I could hear some low voices and sounds of activity beyond the carriage. I quietly opened the door and climbed out.

It was a fine day. Reimer's Hall was on the crest of a hill, with the awakening town spreading out below us, the early workers already beginning to appear on the street. In the other direction, it was country. Birds chirped above, the sun shone, the breeze ruffling the grass was pleasantly refreshing, not cold. The odor of coffee and bacon tantalized me. Looking around, I saw an open fire, around which half a dozen people had gathered, eating and drinking, like a pack of gypsies. Mr. Daugherty was amongst them, quite a gypsy baron, being the only one in a proper shirt and jacket. When he saw me, he got a cup of coffee and came towards me.

"Good morning, ma'am. You had no trouble last night?"

"No, none, though I am considerably worried those two gentlemen might return."

"Not a chance of it. They were so thoroughly disguised they would not know where to go looking if they wanted to. They won't remember a thing, and will take it for a dream if they do."

"I hope you may be right. The thing is, Mr. Daugherty, we find ourselves financially embarrassed."

"'Tis no unusual occurrence hereabouts, ma'am. I'm in the basket myself. April told me of your mishap. Typical for the innkeeper to rob you, then threaten to call in the constable. You are welcome to join us as far as London, but I must ask you to work for your keep. Fiddler's pay is all I can offer—thanks and wine."

"What, no food?"

He took this for a prime joke. "Oh aye, peck and booze was my meaning. Food and drink, but you must realize the others would resent it if you didn't pay the piper, you see. Already Phoebe is making noises about her carriage . . ."

"She is welcome to it. Truth to tell, I am not accustomed to red satin bedding."

"I recognized you for a first-class act."

"Oh, muslin is all we require!" I told him, wondering what this man would consider classier than satin. "Naturally we are willing to work. I would be happy to do what I can, but Miss Brodie must under no account appear again on the stage."

"You?" he asked, staring. "I—I don't think *you* are just our sort, ma'am. No offence meant I assure you, but . . ."

It was only my charge who was first-class, I deduced. "None taken. I did not mean to imply I either sing or act, sir. I am a fair stitcher, however, and would be happy to help out in that capacity."

"Oh," he said, with very little interest, "I have a

44

wardrobe mistress already. Min, Miss Cork, tends to our costume needs. I cannot afford two."

We strolled to a couple of large rocks, which we used as chairs for our outdoor breakfast. I tried the coffee, but found it quite simply undrinkable. I swear it had been boiling an hour. Every bit of bitterness had been allowed to steep out of it. An irridescent slick of oil glimmered on its surface. "You could certainly use a cook," I mentioned, emptying the cup on the ground.

"You cook?" he asked, with very definite interest at this absurd idea.

"A little," I told him. "When I was following the drum. My father was an army man, a captain."

"That would be helpful. We could save a deal of blunt if we could eat more of our meals on the spot. Eating at inns is the killer. There'd be no *haute cuisine* called for. Bread, cheese, wine—fruit, now that summer is coming on, with an occasional hot meal if you can manage it."

"Stew and soup," I mentioned, with a look at their single pot.

"Ah, that'd be grand. Real stew. A rare treat. Will you give it a run, then?"

"I would be happy to, and Perdita can help me."

"There is where I fear we will come to cuffs. Only you will cook."

"That was not my meaning!"

"It is mine," he said simply. "I am not running a charity show. We have to make ends meet. The girl is a good drawing card, a regular canary, and it will only be till we get to London, you know. A couple more stops. What difference will it make?"

We were not so very far removed from Swindon yet that I could feel safe. By nightfall we would be farther removed. It did not seem likely that any of Sir Wilfrid's friends would enter such an establishment as Tuck's. We were desperate, and if Perdita could sing us to London, it must be done, but under her stage name, of course.

"How long will it take us to get there?" I asked, after a frowning pause.

"Four days. We have still to play Kingsclere, Farnborough, possibly Woking, and we are home. If the Woking deal falls through, it will be one less. We move on as soon as breakfast is over, to get set up for tonight at Kingsclere, a small hall only. We won't break even, but will be less in debt than if we omitted it."

"There is nothing for it then but to go along. If those men should show up again . . ."

"O'Reilly will show 'em the door. He's a good lad. You'd be recognizing the Warder, from last night's play."

"He is not the only thing about the play that is familiar."

"You recognized my source, did you?"

"Yes, and most of the lines, to say nothing of the songs. Why did you change the name?"

"The title is too well known. Folks want originality, do you see? They remember Gay's title, and think they don't want to see *The Beggar's Opera again,* but they don't recognize it, or care, once they are in. I've never had to give a refund, in any case. We do a mighty fine *Tempest* as well, but I call it *Stormy Passage,* and leave out some characters."

I figured it was Caliban who was lumbering towards us, also the Warder, O'Reilly. He was a dark-haired, hulking brute of a fellow, holding a loaf of bread between his hairy hands, and gnawing at it as he advanced. "I'll make you known to the folks," Daugherty said, evading the newcomer.

We went to the fireside, where I was presented to several common strangers, whose first business was to discover my name. In the interest of as much privacy as possible, I told them Molly, which pleased the Irish amongst them, of which there were several.

46

They did not ask my last name, nor did I volunteer one. O'Reilly took the notion I was his own private property, and asserted his claim by putting his ham hands around my waist and lifting me a yard into the air. I told him if he ever touched me again, I would pour scalding water over him, which he took as a good token of success with me.

"O'Reilly is a fine lad, but he never can keep his hands off a pretty woman," Daugherty told me, somewhat belatedly. "That is the worst, indeed the only vice in him." He was mistaken there, but that will come out soon enough.

I demanded an apron, and told O'Reilly he might feel free to leave as soon as he had finished eating, as I was busy.

He gave me a not very clean dish wiper, which I tucked into my skirt band, then I dumped the gritty black mess they called coffee on the ground and made up fresh, in the black open pot that hung over the fire. "It's a good cuppa tay we ought to be having," O'Reilly said sadly.

I sliced the three remaining loaves of bread, holding O'Reilly off from them by a menacing flourish of the knife every time his fingers made for the plate. "Sure and you can't feed a grown man on *crumbs,* woman," he told me. His next ploy was to send the monkey to steal some for him. The monkey was called Cathleen, and got away with three slices before I realized from the circle of smiles around me what was afoot, and gave Cathleen the back of my hand across her haunches. She made a very angry, human face.

"Cathleen is jealous of you," O'Reilly told me.

"Does she usually do the cooking? The coffee tasted like it," I replied, knowing by that time O'Reilly was responsible for the brew.

"That's it."

There was neither butter nor cheese. Coffee with sugar and cream from a nearby farm and dry bread

47

was their fare. They seemed satisfied with it, as I was myself. The open air and the picnic atmosphere lent a novelty, almost a charm to the scene.

The show people, always with the exception of Phoebe, were friendly, warm, and totally depraved. It was not my intention to exclude Phoebe from the depravity, actually. She was probably the worst of a bad lot, but I was not immediately exposed to her. Queen Phoebe, as she was referred to in the group, had her meal carried to the door of her traveling bed by Mr. Daugherty. He entered the carriage, too, though I saw very clearly she opened the door wearing her petticoat, and nothing else.

"Mick is sweet-talking Queen Phoebe," O'Reilly informed me. Undaunted by my rough treatment of him, he seldom was more than a foot away from me. He was handy for lifting the heavy pot and keeping the fire stoked up. The actors *did* use some hot water for their morning ablutions, which I was relieved to see, though I think the better part of it was for the men's shaving. They would each bring a small pot of water and sit it on the edge of the fire. There were more pots than I first thought, but the constant movement of the caravan kept things in a state of confusion.

I took a cup of coffee and a slice of bread to Perdita, and asked O'Reilly to bring me a basin of hot water after we had got the beds pushed back into the seats, to make room. He also found a length of muslin from the wardrobe mistress, which we tore in two to use for facecloths and towels. It was like trying to bathe in a shoebox. This done, I returned to the fire to rinse out the coffee cups, and leave them in the sun to dry. There was no soap to be had.

About an hour after he had entered Phoebe's carriage, Mr. Daugherty came out, looking tired and dishevelled. He winked broadly at O'Reilly, thinking I had not seen him, but I am not so young or innocent as to be unaware what went forth, particularly when I saw his breeches hanging on the door handle on the far side of the carriage when I went to Perdita. If men must behave like animals, however, it is best they do it with others of their own sort, and not with the likes of Perdita, to whom he was attentive when not cajoling the Queen.

After an hour or so, everyone was ready to leave. The costumes were crated, the few bits of scenery dismantled and put into a carriage. My cooking pot held our food and cutlery and cups. "What are we waiting for?" I asked Mr. Daugherty, for I was eager to get on closer at least to London.

"Phoebe has not come out yet," he told me. That was it. We sat around looking at each other till the Queen stepped out of her drawing room, outfitted as yesterday in the ostrich plumes and the sable wrap, which was seen, in broad daylight, to be infested with moth holes and of uncertain coloring. She was a fine looking woman, for all that. She was close to thirty, I estimated, full-figured, with handsome, striking features, black hair, dark eyes, a large nose and a broad smile.

"I will take my constitewtional now," she told Daugherty, who nodded his approbation. She paced up and down the meadow, all alone, for perhaps ten minutes, her skirts riling up the dust, and picking up bits of dead grass and burrs as she went. It was really a comical sight to see her so stately and grand in a meadow, insisting on this perquisite she had gained for herself, of holding up business while she walked

Perdita sat with me on my rock, waiting. When Phoebe was tired, she walked up to us in her grandest manner and stopped. An icy smile was levelled at us. "You girls are new, if I am not mistaken?" she asked, in a parody of graciousness. She was the monarch, greeting new subjects.

"You met April yesterday, Phoebe," Daugherty reminded her.

"So I did. I had forgotten," she said, to show us how little she cared for the competition. "Mick mentioned your number went over fairly well last night, dear," she said, narrowing her eyes for a good examination of my charge's youthful face.

"Everybody clapped," Perdita answered simply.

"Your first show?"

"Yes."

"And what do *you* do, miss?" she asked, turning her attention to me.

"I cook," I said, and laughed at the absurdity of it.

"With your looks and manners you could play a lady," she volunteered. "Not the ingenew . . ." she added, with an assessing study of my face.

"Oh I am coming to think the role of a lady beyond me," I told her, weak with trying to control my features.

"I don't know about that. You managed to fool Mick," she said, letting some of her spite intrude into her tone. Then she snapped her dark eyes at us and paced off to announce she was ready to leave.

"There's trouble brewing," O'Reilly warned me. "You want to keep your little princess away from the Queen's man, or she'll scratch your eyes out."

"The problem will be to keep the man away from April."

"Phoebe will be no end of help to you. She throws her skirts at every lad that passes by, but only let her catch Mick winking, and she swears she'll leave the show. She once had an offer at the Garden, according to legend. She threatens to accept it when he cuts up stiff, but I doubt their memories are so long in London that they recall the offer."

Phoebe and Daugherty drove in the blue lead carriage; Perdita and I were jammed into another with about six other girls, one of whom was the blond Angie, Perdita's informative friend.

The talk along the way does not bear repeating. It was of men, money, failed opportunities and unlikely hopes for future stardom or mistress-ship under a wealthy patron. Angie knew a girl who was being kept "in a *grand* establishment with a piano" by a *lord,* and another who had a "regular arrangement with a Cit," which allowed her to bank a hundred guineas per annum. There was really very little mention of acting. Their greater hope for success was rooted in selling themselves to the highest bidder. It was a pity our lecherous visitor last night had not made his offer to one of these girls. I cannot think he would have had the least difficulty in attaching any one of them.

Perdita sat with her ears flapping and her eyes like saucers, lapping up the disreputable stories. I had little hope that any of it was passing over her head. Her questions indicated quite clearly she knew what sort of "regular arrangement" Angie's friend had made. I wonder where the young girls learn so much nowadays. I only heard the facts of life from a married friend when I was twenty-one, and even then I did not believe the half of it.

Our caravan made poor time, harnessed as it was to teams that had much in common with my old jade, Ginger. Daugherty treated us to luncheon at a very inferior inn, where we occupied the entire common room. We dined on sausages, potatoes, cabbage and ale. O'Reilly told me in a quiet aside that he would "be good for a bottle of wine" if I liked, but I could not like to sink too deep into his debt, knowing by this time how debts were discharged in the group between a female and a male. I drank my ale.

"Ye've a touch of class, lassie," he complimented me. "Aye, and added a gloss of it to your gel, too," he added, glancing along the board to where Perdita was daintily cutting her sausage, and eating at a more decorous pace than the others, who gobbled up the food as though they were at a trough.

When we returned to the caravan, our large cooking pot was the recipient of three spoons and a fork,

51

pulled out from under O'Reilly's shirt. I mentioned earlier he had another vice than chasing women. "O'Reilly is on the nab lay," Angie explained, when my eyes widened at his felonious behavior. "He has nabbed half the snow we own."

"Snow?" I asked.

"Linens," he explained, "but I've let up on the ken lay since joining Tuck's."

"Since you spent a fortnight in the roundhouse, you mean," Angie laughed. O'Reilly had been caught breaking and entering a gentleman's house the year before, but had bribed his way out of it.

We arrived at Kingsclere late in the afternoon. I hoped we would be sleeping at an inn, but when I dropped a hint to Daugherty, he said it "would depend on the gate," which meant on how much money he collected at the evening's performance. The whole show was run on that short a shoestring. Strictly hand to mouth. If it happened to rain to keep the coves at home, it seemed we would be without peck and booze on the morrow. Everyone watched the sky very closely, becoming irritable if a cloud passed overhead. Daugherty gave me a guinea and told me to buy supper for us all, something I could serve cold, or cook over an open fire. While I took Perdita to go to the shops, the rest of them continued on to the hall, which was pointed out to us on the main street of the town.

O'Reilly was our footman and bodyguard. He was about six feet four inches tall, and very broad. He had crisp black hair and a moustache. I was grateful for his help in selecting the food, for I had really no idea what to get. He picked up a dozen loaves of bread, cheese, coffee, while I sneaked a couple of dozen of eggs and butter into the box. I do not infer I hid my things from the store clerk, but only from O'Reilly. Bacon he decided was too much trouble, but a leg of smoked ham was added to our supplies when we discovered we had some money left over.

"You ladies run on over to the hall, while I see about a tank of ale from the inn. You'd best slip these into your pocket for me, Mol," he added, sliding half a dozen cigars from under his shirt. "In case they send a search after me. I think the lad saw me lift them."

"Mr. O'Reilly, you have been at it again!"

"A bonus we call it. They raise their prices for us, as we're not regular customers."

"You'll end up in gaol!"

"Not if you get them into your pocket," he said impatiently. I took them and ran as fast as I could to the hall.

There was a general circus going forth there. The piano player was trying out the instrument, while Phoebe bellowed out a song, for she wished to test the "acewstics" before the nightly show. The wardrobe mistress was hanging up outfits and looking for nails to hold the curtains that would form temporary dressing rooms.

Seeing Daugherty sitting with his feet up on another chair and his head relaxed against the wall, resting, I accosted him.

"Where are all the girls?" I asked, for there were about half a dozen of them missing.

"Walking the streets, trying to stir up a little excitement to draw customers in tonight. Why don't you take April for a walk?"

"I am afraid we might be arrested," I said, with a thought to the stolen cigars.

"She hasn't been soliciting openly?" he asked sharply.

"What?"

"I don't want you girls soliciting on the streets. The law takes a dim view of that in these small towns. Let 'em come to you after the show."

"Mr. Daugherty!" I gasped, struck rigid at his speech. He thought we were *streetwalkers!* Here I thought he knew we were truly ladies in distress,

53

but it was no such a thing. Like Phoebe, he thought *acting* like ladies was our business.

"Now don't fly into the boughs, Molly. I haven't said a word, but you and I know the score. Your girl is worth a pretty penny. Don't sell her here. Take her up to London, where she'll be appreciated, and fetch a good price."

"You despicable . . ."

He hunched his shoulders, as though to indicate I was acting still, and none too convincingly either. Then he lifted his curled beaver from his knees, put it over his eyes, and ignored me. I stormed off, to see Perdita practicing a few dance steps in the corner with Angie. She had her skirt hiked up to her knees, and was laughing, looking not very different from the real lightskirts, only much prettier. Dangerously pretty.

When O'Reilly arrived, I had him take the food to a little room behind the main auditorium. I gave him his cigars, without a word, but with a darkly accusing look. While I sliced the bread and buttered it, he ate half the ham, and drank a glass of ale, then put his two arms around me and tried to kiss me. Luckily, I still held the bread knife.

The Queen deigned to come amongst us commoners for dinner, but sat a little apart, glaring at Perdita and myself and whispering sweet words into Daugherty's ears. I believe she was the source of his opinion about us, but really his opinion did not matter, as long as he meant to help me protect my valuable charge and get her to London in a chaste condition. We were no sooner finished eating than it was time for the actors to begin their preparations. I did not leave, as I meant to oversee Perdita's dressing, and ensure she did not go on the stage again in a flimsy red rag. It was rather exciting, watching them put on their makeup and costumes, and strut to and fro, practicing their lines.

"I want a different outfit for April," I told Daugherty.

Of course he knew our real names, but was always careful to use our new ones, and so was I.

"The red suited her. It was beautiful."

"No, it was cheap and vulgar. She need not look like a trollop."

"Maybe you're right," he said, looking to where she stood, across the room, with some other girls. "She could lend us a touch of class. Let's see what Min can do."

We sought out Miss Cork. She was a thin, aging, wizened little bit of a thing, resembling a ferret. She led us to the trunks of unused materials and gowns. We rifled together happily enough, finally settling on a blue silk gown with a spangled skirt.

"Dorothy Nolan wore this in *Tempest*—Mick called it something else," she told me. "We did a musical version of it. She was Miranda. She looked fine, got taken up by a Member of Parliament. She was my girl, you know. He very nearly married her."

"You daughter, Min?" I asked, for she was called, you remember, Miss Cork.

"Oh no, my girl, like April and you. She could have had him legal if she'd listened to me, and held out a little longer. Used to send her flowers and jewels, followed the show halfway around England, but in the end she gave in and became his mistress. Your girl will do well too, Molly. I don't doubt she'll get herself set up with a noble patron. What will *you* do? Stay with her, or get a new girl?"

"Stay with her," I said, as some answer must be made, and there was no point in voicing our worthiness forever.

"You're wise. Don't let her toss you over. You ought to get her to sign a contract for you. Daugherty always does. You're the one guiding her, and you deserve something for it. Dorothy didn't give me a cent, but she came running back to me fast enough when her M.P. was through with her. The fellows will always try to be rid of the bawd, though. They're wicked about it. Selfish brutes. I'll heat up the iron and give this blue a press. It should look well on April."

I took Perdita to a private room to change, and arranged her coiffure myself to a tidier do than she had worn the night before. When all was done, I went to the back of the hall to watch the show again. It was still amusing, perhaps more so now that I was a little acquainted with the performers. Things that had gone unnoticed the night before were obvious, after listening to the girls' complaints. Phoebe's hogging of the stage, the manner in which she contrived to upstage Angie when they were together, her trick of delaying her entrance to heighten interest, all were noticed and enjoyed. Even when she was in the background, she held attention by some trick or other. She had a million of them. Movement was the main one. When Daugherty and Angie were speaking, she ought to have faded into the background, but she would fiddle with her hair, run her hands down the sides of her waist, or move about to pick up some object. It was amusing, too, to realize the "jewelry" the fence handled was of the very cheapest variety, while they spoke of diamonds and gold. The colonel's uniform too was threadbare and falling apart under the arms. Min patched it as often as Phoebe's seams, but it looked well on the stage.

I kept a close eye on the audience as well, my main interest to discover the two city bucks. I was vastly relieved they did not come. They had forgotten the pocket Venus. Without them to incite the audience to a frenzy, her three songs passed with no more than a thunderous ovation.

Chapter Five

"Did you make enough money to afford rooms at the inn, Mick?" I asked when I went behind stage to gather up my charge. It seemed pretentious to go on calling him Mr. Daugherty when the lowliest prompter used his first name.

"We've decided it's best to sleep in the carriages while the fine weather holds up," he answered. "The deal with Woking is not firm, and if it falls through, we'll need the few pounds taken tonight for food."

It was hard to press for the luxury of a room and bed when the very food to sustain us was at question. "We'll go to the carriage now, then," I answered, trying not to show my disappointment.

"Why do you not stick around for the party?" he asked. "There'll be a few fellows come round to the Green Room. O'Reilly has some ale standing by. The celebration will be good for you and the girl, Molly."

I knew the girl would like it well enough—too well. I refused, gently but firmly. O'Reilly, billowing clouds of foul-smelling smoke from the stolen cigars, came to add his entreaties to the manager's. Already the party was assembling, no *haut ton* affair, to judge from the provincials in ill-cut jackets, their heads reeking of lavender water and their breath of intoxicating liquor.

I went to break the sad news to Perdita that we were leaving. "We cannot go yet, Molly," she said, peering all around the hall. I felt in my bones she was looking for the gentlemen who had paid her such attention the night before.

"They are not here," I told her.

"I know. I couldn't find out who they are, either. Angie did not know them, and if Phoebe does, she won't tell us. Min thinks they are *lords*."

"They were as drunk as the proverbial lord, at least. Come along."

"I told you we cannot go yet."

"Why not?"

She reached up and whispered her reason in my ear. Even to this shameless hussy, it was a matter to be kept close. How do I tell you without causing you to close the book and throw it into the flames as a pernicious document? Hold on to your chair. The reason is that Angie was entertaining a male in our bedroom. It was strictly a business transaction; she wanted money, needed it for some necessity or other, and was plying her old trade to acquire it. This being the case, the Green Room seemed suddenly less undesirable. Even Mr. Croft was coming to appear in a better light.

"I have a good mind to send a note off to your father to come and take us home," I said, pink to the ears.

"Oh no, Molly. *This* is only for a few more days. Mr. Croft would be forever."

"Let us find a quiet, dark corner, then, and wait till Angie is finished with her—her business."

Perdita accepted the command in theory, but in fact, she cast such bold and inviting smiles over her naked shoulder that we were not long alone in our private corner. Half a dozen under-bred males came

58

trotting over to ply her with stares, ale, compliments, and propositions. I did not escape entirely myself. A person in a snuff-colored jacket and green waistcoat, the oldest and seediest of the lot, actually, asked me frankly, "How much?" For what, you may imagine. He was quite insistent, too. In desperation, I beckoned to O'Reilly, who made short shrift of him.

"Better take the hint, Mister, 'fore you get the kick," was his polite manner of explaining the situation.

This disgusting interlude caused me to divert my attention from Perdita for a moment. The man who fancied myself his type was not small. Half full of liquor, he was ready to invite O'Reilly to step outside. My hope was to prevent outright violence, which would bring the constable down on our heads. Mick paced the hall, alert for just such difficulty as I was causing. He paced towards us, and when he learned the nature of the wrangle, said softly aside to me, "Why do you not oblige him, Mol? You wanted a room for the night. Here is your chance. You can keep your fee. We have no contract signed."

"I don't want a room that badly, sir," I told him.

When O'Reilly finally got rid of the man, I turned back to see Perdita wearing a radiant smile. She was not making sport of my predicament, but smirking at someone across the room. I looked to see what hedgebird she was encouraging, and found myself gazing at the city buck from last night. He was alone this time, having left his friend behind. He was again outfitted in his elegant black evening clothes, jacket and pantaloons. His eyes rested on Perdita, transfixed. He was not so intoxicated on this occasion. He was not flushed, or stumbling, but striding towards her at a rapid gait. I looked about in alarm for some spot to hide her, and found none.

Suddenly he was there, at our side, making a

graceful bow, smiling, devouring her with his blue eyes. "Hello, April," he said, in a besotted voice.

"Good evening, sir. You have the advantage of me. I do not know *your* name," she answered, with a bold smile, while lifting the big ostrich fan to bat at him in a playful way.

"Mr. Brown, at your service, ma'am," he replied, repeating his bow.

"Another Mr. Brown!" I said hastily, inserting myself between the two of them. "What a popular name it is hereabouts. I have not met a thing but Joneses and Browns all night long." Naturally the men did not dare to give their real names, any more than we did ourselves.

He cast one annoyed flicker of a glance at me, before stepping aside to get at Perdita. "This is my chaperone, Molly," she told him.

"Delighted, ma'am," he said, again just barely glancing at me. "May I join you?" he went on, turning back to the Incomparable.

"We don't charge for the use of a chair," was her saucy reply, picked up from Queen Phoebe.

"I wager you charge plenty for—other privileges," he said boldly, occupying the chair beside her.

Phoebe was moving across the hall, playing off her old tricks to attract attention, but without any luck whatsoever. I looked in alarm to see where I should station myself, either on Perdita's other side, or his. I judged him to be the more dangerous, and darted to get the chair, just beating Phoebe to it by a hair. I fully expected his next comment would be to inquire the price of those "other privileges." He was more refined than the snuff-coated man. "I am desolate to have missed your performance this evening," he was saying. "I was obliged to attend a very dull party. I hope you are flattered to learn I have dashed twenty-five miles to be here."

"Where is your friend tonight?" Perdita asked,

while the hovering Phoebe was on the alert for his reply.

"Come now, *that* is not what I want to hear! Never mind my friend. You are wearing a different gown this evening. I preferred you in red. It suited you better."

"Molly thought it was vulgar," she told him, with a pouting face to myself.

Phoebe made some ill-natured remark about red suiting the little princess, if it was vulgarity that was in style, and flounced off to Mick, without Mr. Brown's even being aware she had been near him.

"How can you say so, Molly?" he asked, showing me a surprised quizzical smile.

I opened my lips to reply, but was looking at the back of his head. "Isn't there somewhere we can go to be alone?" I overheard him say. I had to lean forward to catch the low words.

I was on my feet. "April is not leaving," I told him sternly.

His lips clenched into a frustrated, thin line. "It seems I must deal with *you* first, Molly. Excuse us, April. I shall be right back. Don't go away."

He arose, took me by the elbow to march a few yards beyond Perdita's hearing, then stopped. "Save your breath, Mr. Brown. April is not leaving this room," I told him.

"I do not mean to quibble about terms. I am generous, and I am in a hurry. I want to get her out of here before you reach London."

"Forget it. Just go away; leave her alone."

"You won't make a better deal elsewhere."

"I am not trying to negotiate a *deal*."

"Is she already taken? I cannot believe you would be traveling with this band of gypsies if it were the case. Tell me what arrangement is in the offing, and I shall undo it."

"You misunderstand the situation entirely."

"No, ma'am, I don't. I am not quite a greenhorn in

affairs of this sort. You have got yourself a diamond of the first water. Naturally, you want top pound for her. I am willing to come down heavy. Just state your finder's fee, and I shall do the rest, arrange a generous settlement on the girl. Say, a thousand a year during pleasure, and half that sum upon disagreement, or until she is placed elsewhere. But with a time limit of one year. I don't want to be tied up with a pension."

This offhand speech, placing Perdita in the light of a piece of merchandise for hire, and myself as a flesh-broker nearly robbed me of rational speech. "I wish you will talk sense!" was all I could think of to say in refutation.

"Well, make a counter offer," was his astonished reply. Perhaps the offer *was* generous, as these matters go. "*Naturally* I mean to carry all the costs of her establishment, and so on. She will be safe, and well cared for with me. I can supply character references, if you fear I mean to abuse the girl."

"I cannot think character references for a Mr. Brown would be at all enlightening," I answered in a voice of heavy irony.

His eyes narrowed in quick suspicion. He was silent a moment, probably considering whether it were safe to tell me his real name. He looked back towards Perdita, who smiled and waved her fingers at him. Such an expression came over his face, a foolish, fatuous, lecherous, eager smile. He turned slowly back to me.

"Any contract you have with the girl would not be valid, Molly. She is obviously a minor. I don't know what she may mean to you . . ."

"A great deal."

"Relative? Niece, sister—what? Are you her legal guardian?"

"Yes," I said at once, to bolster my claim. "She is my responsibility, and she is not ripe for the sort of life you are interested in procuring for her."

"She won't make a ripple on the stage, if that is what you have in mind. She has beauty, but no voice, and no histrionic ability."

"That need not concern you."

"It doesn't. Your being with this traveling whorehouse tells me very clearly what you both are. Now, cut line and let us arrange the business, or I shall bypass you in the negotiations entirely. It does not do to be too greedy, and as to your alleged guardianship, you are quite obviously unfit for it. I cannot think your character would stand up in court."

I was at *point non plus*. I could not dare to tell him the truth, reveal our real names, and nothing else would convince him we were anything but what we seemed. I saw, from the corner of my eye, Angie saunter in the door, pinning up her hair and straightening her gown. Our carriage was free now. We could leave, but first I had to get rid of Mr. Brown, so he did not see where we went. Looking around the hall, I caught O'Reilly's eye. He came forward at an imploring look from me.

"What can I do for you, Molly my lass?" he asked in a hearty, cheerful voice, but he was measuring Mr. Brown's shoulders as he spoke, ready to treat him as roughly as was called for.

"Mr. Brown is being a nuisance, O'Reilly," I said. "He would like to leave, but cannot find the door."

"Come along, lad. If the lady says no, she means no. Molly don't mince words. She speaks right on." He clamped one of his hairy hamhocks on Brown's elegant shoulder, and lifted him bodily from the floor. You never saw such an astonished face in your life as Mr. Brown wore. I could not suppress a smile, and didn't try very hard, either.

O'Reilly dropped his opponent so hard the floor shook. While Brown was still on his way to the ground, he turned around and let a quick jab flash into O'Reilly's stomach. A pained howl and a curse were emitted simultaneously. The quick jab was followed by a blow to O'Reilly's jaw. I stood by horrified as Daugherty came darting forward to join the fray. Within seconds, the rest of the party had formed a ring around the fighters, like boys watching a dogfight. I did not wait to see more, but pulled Perdita out of the ring and towards the door. The sounds behind us indicated a free-for-all was fast developing. We went to the carriage, got in, and sat shivering on the banquettes.

"I hope he doesn't know we're here," I said. "If he comes looking for you, Perdita, I mean to knock him out. In fact, I am going to get a weapon this instant." I checked the door of the hall to see no one was coming out, before jumping out of the carriage to look around in the darkness. I found a stout tree-branch and a large rock. There we sat in the carriage, holding our makeshift weapons, while Perdita giggled and crowed over her conquest.

"He came twenty-five miles to see me."

"It is nothing to boast of. The man is a hardened rake. His sort ought to be behind bars, and not walking loose to pester innocent women. If I were not afraid of the publicity, I would lodge a complaint against him."

"I think he's handsome."

"He's a regular Don Juan."

"Oh but I always wanted to tame a rake. If he knew who I really am, he would be interesed in more than a mistress-ship. He would marry me."

"Would he not make a fine, upstanding husband? You would not be subjected to much of his company, at any rate. He'd be out burning up the countryside, squandering his fortune on a new lightskirt every season."

"How much did he offer?"

"I shan't insult you by saying."

"A gent once offered Phoebe two hundred a year, plus paying for all her expenses."

The vulgar "gent" annoyed me as much as the rest

64

of her speech. "Generous!" I said sardonically. It would not do to flatter her with the sum after this revelation. She might take into her head to accept the offer. Anything seemed possible in this demi-monde we had fallen into.

We sat for a long time, watching, waiting, talking, with me trying to get some propriety into her head, and herself oblivious to anything but the glory of having had a degrading offer from a rake.

It was our new custom to sleep in our petticoats, but I could not like to be so scantily-clad in case we were hauled from the flimsy safety of our carriage. We kept our gowns on our backs till Mr. Brown came out. I had hoped to see him flung from the door headfirst, as he deserved, but Daugherty was keen to keep any altercation to a minimum, because of the law. When Brown came out, Mick accompanied him. They had reached the best of terms. Mick had his arm flung around the man's shoulder, their heads together, talking.

"He's trying to press Phoebe on him," Perdita said, in a voice of pique.

"An ideal match. I wish him luck."

I began to think the girl was right. The two men went into the blue carriage, Phoebe's red satin place of business. Mick would take a discreet departure, and Phoebe would slip in. This was not quite what happened. The men entered the carriage, stayed for about a quarter of an hour, during which Phoebe did not join them. Then Brown came out and walked away, whistling merrily, while Daugherty stood at the carriage door, looking after him, and patting his pocket in a satisfied way that suggested he had got money out of the scoundrel.

When Brown was safely away, I went out to speak to Daugherty. "What happened? How did you get rid of him?"

"Never underestimate the power of persuasion, Molly my girl. I talked him out of it."

"Yes, but how?"

He put his head back and laughed. "I told him April will be a mother in half a year, and he was amazingly eager to forget her. His sort don't want a by-blow around their necks. Why, 'twould be enough to give a lad a bad name."

One becomes accustomed to even violent shocks after a while. I had learned so many strange, debauched things during the past days that my only reaction was amusement, even admiration at his quick thinking. "You are up to all the rigs, Mick. Now why didn't *I* think of that?"

"Because you are not up to snuff, Mol. Why, I begin to think you need a keeper yourself."

"I still don't see how you got money out of him for telling him. Never mind trying to con me, Mick. I saw you patting your pocket. How much did you get? Enough to hire a room at the inn?"

"Devil a bit of it. He gave me a guinea for recommending a female to him, one of my ex-girls who has set up trade in London."

"I hope he goes directly to her, and never darkens the door of our theater again."

"That's exactly what he plans. Don't worry your pretty head he'll be pestering April."

As he spoke, his arm went around my shoulders, his hand falling rather low on my chest. "Well, the night's young, and the brat is tucked up safe in her bed. What do you say you and I . . ." He looked over his shoulder at the blue carriage, then back to me, with a wary half smile.

I should have beat him, or kicked him, or at least expressed a decent Christian outrage. Perhaps it was my relief at his having got rid of Brown for us that mitigated my wrath. "I don't think so, Mick," was all I said. I tried to hold in my giggles till I got inside our own carriage, without quite succeeding. He hunched his shoulders philosophically, and re-entered the Green Room to try his luck elsewhere, while Perdita and I finally undressed for the night. We curled up, one on each banquette of the carriage, with pillows behind us and a blanket on top. It was not so uncomfortable as you might imagine, though I *was* longing for a long soak in a tub, and some clean clothing.

Chapter Six

The remainder of our stay with Tuck's Traveling Theater was relatively uneventful, but only relatively so. Prior to leaving home, cooking over an open fire, singing on the stage, helping O'Reilly rob stores and being propositioned by provincial squires would have been something of an event in our quiet, respectable lives. It was the relief of having at last lost Mr. Brown that made our other activities seem tame in comparison. He was not on hand at Farnborough nor at Woking, which deal Daugherty closed successfully.

I began to see there was something in O'Reilly's claim that the shopkeepers raised their prices for us. When we went to buy our food at Farnbrough, we had a female serve us, a rather handsome lady with an eye for O'Reilly. The two of them bantered and flirted while the purchases were made, but when she weighed our ham, her thumb came down heavy on the scales, while her flashing eyes diverted his attention. When I saw her tallying up seven and a half pounds for a piece of meat that weighed five without her help, I was not slow to scoop a handful of cigars up for my friend, and conceal them in my skirt pocket. He was too besotted with her eyes to do it for himself.

"A handsome woman," he said as we walked back to the hall.

"As handsome a hussy as ever pushed her thumb on the scales," I told him.

"Did she now? Ah well, a body has to live, Mol," he said leniently. "We all need to look out for ourselves —you and me and the shopkeepers. A man needs food, and love. The *food's* been grand since you joined us."

"Have the girls not been treating you well?"

"Ye know I don't care for none of them fireships. Who else would I be giving this to but you?" he asked, pulling a very ugly little statuette out of his pocket. It was of Cupid, holding a bow in one hand, and a heart in the other. I had seen it before, about five minutes ago, on the shelf of the shop. It had not been amongst our purchases. He nabbed it from the shelf, while rolling his eyes at the clerk.

"I didn't forget you either, O'Reilly," I told him, taking the gimcrack thing, and giving him his cigars. "I believe we broke even on that deal. I didn't know how many cigars to nab, but as I was ciphering in my mind, I don't believe I took enough."

"You're coming on grand," he praised.

"Thank you. I daresay I have been cheated in the shops all my life, without realizing it."

O'Reilly stole other things, too. Eggs never purchased appeared for breakfast, and once a lovely green goose, certainly removed from a neighborhood wall, where it had been hanging, but he never got caught at it. I chided him for stealing when the victim had no chance to retaliate, like the shopkeepers.

"Don't half the village sneak in after we stop guarding the door?" he pointed out. "We sold a hundred and twenty-three tickets last night, and everyone of the two hundred seats was full before the show was over. Fair's fair."

70

His original bookkeeping in the field of ethics was difficult to refute, though I do not mean to say I think it was *right*.

Business was good enough that we could sleep in a cheap inn that night, which also allowed us the luxury of washing our linens and taking a bath, and sleeping in a bed, but unfortunately we had to share our room with Angie and another actress, who snored.

In the morning, we were off on the last lap to London. The crew spoke of "Mother Gaines's" as being the place we would put up there. "Where is this place, O'Reilly?" I asked my faithful companion, as we sat over breakfast at the inn before leaving. "In fact, *what* is it?"

"A rough and tumbling boardinghouse in the east end of the city. You'll find many traveling troupes meeting in that neighborhood this time of the year, readying their show for the summer circuit. There'll be bargaining for work, deciding on shows and costumes. Will you stay on?"

"No, we only stay till London. I have to take April there."

"Aye, so I've heard. And what will you do with yourself then, when the gel is gone?"

"I will go with her."

"Nay, her man won't want that."

"She is not going to a man. That is a nasty rumor I cannot seem to squash."

"She'll find one soon enough," he told me, with a doubting look, still believing I whitewashed our true characters.

I just smiled and shook my head, not wanting to be too informative. "I've a plan to put to you," he said tentatively.

"What is that?"

He drummed his hairy fingers on the table, then suddenly reached out and grabbed my hands in a numbing grip. "Marry me," he said. I blinked a couple of times, while considering what refusal to make to this unexpected proposal. I did not want to hurt O'Reilly's feelings. Of the whole crew, he was my favorite. Warts and all, I appreciated him.

"You're not like the others, lass. You've got spunk, and are dashed pretty, too, beneath your nice as a nun's hens manners. This voyaging life isn't for the likes of you. I'll get a regular job and set you up a cottage. How would you like that, eh?"

"That—that sounds very cosy, O'Reilly," I said, in a high, unnatural voice. I was overcome with emotion. "Actually, I have got a job lined up," I said, to soften the blow.

"Doing what?"

"Nursemaid," I answered, grabbing at the first thought that offered.

He laughed. "That's a new word for what you do. Who is your new girl?"

He clearly thought I meant to set up, or continue, as an abbess. I believe both he and Mick thought I was delivering Perdita to some rich patron in the city. Various remarks they made suggested it.

"Now you wouldn't want me to give away trade secrets," I said, bantering my way out of a real answer.

"Be sure to get her under contract next time."

"What do you mean?"

"Just do what O'Reilly tells you. Sure you won't change your mind, Mol? I meant to do it up right, with a priest and all."

"I'm sure, but I am flattered you asked me." He did not remain long after that.

We arrived at Mother Gaines's boardinghouse in mid-afternoon. My first move upon arrival was to write a note to Alton's, asking John to come and fetch us. I sent it off with the houseboy, giving him the last shilling I had to my name. That accomplished, there was nothing to do but wait for his arrival. There was a large parlor in the house which was used as a common room for the various people putting up *chez* Mother Gaines. One fails to try to imagine what life had produced such a character as Mother Gaines, who took infinite delight in opening her portals to such tag rag and bobtail as were assembled there. She asked no question but the important one; did you have any money? That ascertained, she welcomed you with small ale and small talk, all of it related to the theater. She looked like a gargoyle from some ancient building come to life and painted up with rouge. Some of our group were there, exchanging anecdotes with another traveling show. Others of us had gone shopping, or out for a walk.

Queen Phoebe descended the stairs in her finest raiments, the plate bonnet and ostrich plumes. "Are you going to take your constitewtional now, Phoebe?" Perdita asked. I am not sure whether she poked fun at the girl's pronunciation, or had picked up this vulgar mannerism unconsciously. I think that, in spite of my scorn, she rather admired Phoebe.

I expected some fireworks, as Phoebe still disliked my charge very cordially. But she was in a tolerant mood today. "I've an appointment at the Garden, dear," she said.

"Good luck. I hope you get the job. What role is it?"

"Nothing *you* would be interested in."

"Covent Garden nun," Angie whispered, not quite softly enough.

Phoebe's fine dark eyes sparkled in anger. "We're not *all* in that trade, Angie." Her eyes also stared rather hard at Perdita. "Some of us are able to act, but I think *you* are wise to close with Mr. Brown, April." She swept from the room, her ostrich plumes dancing behind her.

I had hoped I had heard the name of Brown for the last time. I looked uneasily at my charge, wondering if it were possible she had set up some meeting with him behind my back. She only looked amused. "What have you in mind, Angie?" she asked her friend.

73

"If Queen Phoebe really gets an offer from the Garden, Mick says I'll be his new leading lady. If she don't, I'll just go on playing second fiddle."

Mick came over to us. Before we had been chatting for long about the subject that consumed them all—what was to be done next—John Alton was announced.

What a blessed relief it was to see a respectable old friend after our sorry escapade. "What in the deuce are you girls doing in this hole?" he demanded bluntly, with no regard for the others' feelings. "I made sure it was a mistake when I read the address. You ought to know better than to bring Perdie here, Moira."

Mick looked positively alarmed. "Who is this?" he asked.

Meanwhile Perdita had jumped up to greet her neighbor. In her excitement, and with an unsavory use of her new manners, she threw her arms around him.

"Mr. Alton is taking us to stay with friends," I told Daugherty.

"You can't leave yet!"

"That's what you think!" I told him, and went to get our bonnets and pelisses.

He came trotting out to the hallway after me. "You're making a big mistake, Molly," he began, grabbing onto my elbow to detain me. "Alton is nobody. Don't you know who Mr. Brown is?"

"No, but I know what he is, and we are not interested."

"It is all arranged! He'll have my neck in a sling if she's gone."

"Do you mean to stand there and tell me you have cooked up some deal for Brown to come here?" I demanded. "Mick Daugherty, whoever said there were no snakes in Ireland was mistaken! It was done the night you took him into the blue carriage, wasn't it? *Wasn't it?*"

74

"I meant to share the blunt with you. I knew she'd give in to him, sooner or later. No point antagonizing him, and you don't have her under contract. She told me so. He was generous—gave me a hundred pounds. I *have* to produce her."

My first violent burst of anger gave way to mirth. How capital it was, that Mr. Brown had been hoodwinked. So insistent, so overbearing, underhanded, every vile thing you can name, and we were outwitting him. When he came, his April would be gone without a trace, for we would naturally not leave any forwarding address. His staying away from the Green Room for those few nights had been a ruse to calm my nerves, to get the Incomparable safely delivered to London, with no bother or fuss. "You are not going to produce her, Daugherty. Better produce his hundred pounds, instead."

"I've spent half of it. I'll give you the rest."

"No, thanks. Maybe he'll be satisfied with a pound of flesh instead. I know you are familiar with the works of Shakespeare, but I have a variation to suggest. Let him cut out your tongue; it will save you a deal of future trouble."

"Where are you going? Give me the address."

"Send him to Carleton House. If April is not there, he is bound to find some plump bird to his taste."

Alton and Perdita came into the hall. I went to the doorway of the parlor to bid all my old friends a last farewell. My anger with Daugherty robbed me of any feeling of regret at leaving, not that there would be much, but shared adventures had forged a bond between some of us. I felt a pang in particular for Angie, to know she was mired forever in this sort of existence, at such a young age. I must say she looked perfectly content with her lot, though. She was playing with Cathleen, already forgetful of us when we left.

We squeezed into John's stylish sporting curricle and were off, free of all the ignominies of the theatrical world at last. Looking back over my shoulder, I saw Daugherty in the middle of the road, checking to see what route we took. I was sorry John had given his real name, but in the commotion it might have escaped Daugherty's notice. He would not know where in the city to find him in any case. I did not think we would hear of Mr. Brown again.

"Moira, I wish you will tell me what is going on," John said, shouting over the noise of the carriage, the horses, and the busy streets. "I can't make heads or tails of Perdie's story. What were you doing with that pack of pimps and trollops?"

His youthful face was red with annoyance, while his brown eyes bulged with shock. "It is a long story, John. Let us wait till we reach the quiet of your saloon. How is your mama?" How quickly the trite, polite phrases returned to mind.

"Sick as a dog," he answered frankly. "Got a dose of this wicked flu that is going round. Hope I don't pick it up from her, for I am due to attend a house party on the weekend. Leave very soon to go to Grifford's place, in Kent. They are trying to find a *parti* for that ugly patch of a daughter that has been hanging on the family tree till she's wilted. Half the men in London are going to look her over."

"You can't go," Perdita said calmly. "You will have to take us to Brighton instead, to visit my Aunt Maude."

"The devil I will! Millie Grifford may look like a dog, but she is the richest squinter in the country. I'll try my hand with her, like all the others. Favors me, to say the truth. Can't imagine how it came about, for I never paid the least heed to her. Didn't realize she was so rich, till Tony tipped me the clue."

"We can borrow a carriage and team from John, and go to Brighton by ourselves," I said to placate my charge. "John can lend us a footman for safety's sake. The trip can be made in less than a day."

"Brighton, did you say?" John shouted. "Bromley

76

Hall, Grifford's place, is only ten miles from Brighton. I could pop you two off, on down the coast and double back. Mean to say, if Prinney made it in four and a half hours, I can do it in less. Mind we must leave at the crack of dawn, for the extra twenty miles, I shan't arrive till all hours. Daresay old Mrs. Grifford won't care for it, but she'll be tucked between her sheets long before I get there. I can let on I pulled in shortly after dinner."

"I am sorry to put you to so much trouble," I said, while Perdita overrode my gratitude with a pert, "Good, then it is all settled. Is the Prince Regent at his Brighton Pavilion?"

"How the deuce should *I* know where the old whale is?" was John's reply. "I don't swim with his school. Got a piece of excellent news for you, Perdie."

"What is it?" she asked, interested.

"Got taken up by the FHC."

"What is the FHC?"

"What is the FHC?" he asked, then repeated it a few times, in ever rising tones of incredulity, till I was very curious to hear what magnificent honor was his. "Why it is the Four Horse Club. Top of the trees. Dandy outfit, dotted tie, striped waistcoat. You will notice I am driving a team of bays. Had to change my grays in on 'em. Papa, dashed skint, would not buy me another pair, and of course you cannot be driving anything but bays to Salt Hill."

"This looks like a nifty pair of prads," Perdie congratulated him.

As Alton drove us through the lively section of town, Perdita turned a wistful face to me. "Do you think we might stay with Mrs. Alton, instead of going to Brighton, Moira?" she asked.

"No," John answered bluntly, while I jollied her along with tales of the vastly superior company she would enjoy at the seaside resort town.

"We must stay long enough to have some gowns made up, in any case," she pointed out, not without some reason. The gowns in which we sat were closer to rags, well soiled rags at that. "And you must lend me some money, John, for we are flat busted."

"Where did you pick up such an expression?" he asked suspiciously. The language he spoke himself was only nominally the King's English, but he expected better of ladies. Truth to tell, I found myself cropping out into Theater English more often than was prudent. Their jargon was lively and descriptive; it stuck too easily in the memory, to pop out at injudicious moments to betray our recent past.

"Perdita spends too much time in the stables," I said, to fob him off, till I decided how much he must be told.

Chapter Seven

Despite her wicked dose of the flu, Mrs. Alton was not in bed. She sat in her yellow saloon, lounging on a chaise longue, with a pile of white cards by her side, trying to determine the likely duration of her illness, and what cards she could accept. She awaited our arrival, as John had told her he was picking us up. The odd manner of his doing so might have raised a query in a normal mother's breast. Not in Mrs. Alton's. It was her main object in life to attach Perdita and her fortune for her only son. She overlooked every flaw in her darling neighbor; even when the flaw escalated into a huge fault, she was quick to lay the blame in another's dish.

"What a delightful surprise!" she chirped, adjusting the ribbons of an overly ornate cap that held her gray curls in place. She was in her late forties, a plain countrywoman who aped city manners for two months a year, when her squire brought her to London for the Season. "You catch me all at sixes and sevens, my dear. Old Mr. Flu has got hold of me, but I shan't give in. Only let me recuperate for a day or two, and I shall show you all the sights. G'day,

Miss Greenwood," she added, acknowledging my presence.

We made our curtsies from a distance, as we neither of us wished to contract her ailment. "How does your papa go on, and his new bride?"

"Fine," Perdita answered carelessly, while I readied my tale to account for our singular appearance in her saloon. Not a single word of my story was necessary. "We are en route to Aunt Maude in Brighton, and stopped off to visit you for a few days. I hope you don't mind."

"Mind? Why, my dear, I could not be happier. I only mind that I am not well enough to show you the sights immediately, today. But John will be my stand-in," she added at once, with a commanding glance to her son.

"Haven't a second to spare, Mama," he answered very quickly. "Got an appointment with Stultz in half an hour."

"Oh, my dear, I *wish* you would reconsider and see Weston. The whole of London recognizes your man at a glance when you frequent Stultz. Though he *does* give you a very handsome shoulder. Perdita will visit me till your appointment is over."

"Have a date at No. 13 Old Bond after that," John informed her. "Jackson's Parlor, you must know."

"That's all right," Perdita said sweetly. "We want to see a modiste this afternoon in any case, Mrs. Alton. We accidentally left our luggage behind, at Chippenham, and Moira lost all our money, so we must have some new gowns ordered, if you will loan us a few guineas."

Even this unlikely tale raised no eyebrows on the hopeful mother-in-law's face. "I shall call my woman. Put it on my bill," she said grandly. "She has her shop on Old Bond, John. Drop off word we want Miss McGavin to come to us, with some samples of her materials."

She ordered tea, and the three of us chatted while

John dashed off to his tailor, with a casual word over his shoulder that he would be home for dinner, and he was looking forward to hearing what hobble Perdie had fallen into, by Jove, and the story had better be good or he'd turn her over his knee and give her a sound thrashing.

The two of us, Perdita and myself, spent a delightful hour scrubbing the grime of the road from our bodies. We leaned shamelessly on Mrs. Alton's unquestioning charity to borrow linens, dressing gowns and stockings till our outfits had been hastily washed and pressed dry. By the time we returned belowstairs, Miss McGavin had arrived, carrying her samples and fashion magazines in a black patent leather bag. Our own gowns had laundered well enough to preclude requiring an afternoon outfit. What would be necessary was one gown for evening wear. Perdita and Mrs. Alton rifled happily through swatches of silks, lutestrings, muslins and crepes to select outfits unfit for a pre-deb.

"Perdita must wear white, must she not?" I reminded the matron.

"To be sure she must. What a pity. This pink would suit her so well, but she cannot wear colors till she is out. That is not to say you cannot enliven your gowns with flowers and ribbons, my dear," she added, to palliate the blow. "With a little garnishing, a white can look very fashionable." The material chosen was unexceptionable: a white peau de soie, but the quantities of ornament chosen caused a fear my charge would look like a fruit salad on a white plate when the thing was finished.

My hope to curtail the selection to one gown for evening wear prospered. "John is taking us to Brighton the day after tomorrow, you recall. Miss McGavin won't have time for more than one each. Indeed I don't see how she is to get the two made up in such a short space."

"I have a half dozen girls working for me. The city

ain't busy yet. A month from now I could not accommodate you, but it happens I am slack at the moment. These will be ready for you by tomorrow, ladies, in the afternoon, in time for your evening party," the modiste assured us.

I selected for myself a plain gown in pale green silk. Spring was not the season for a more sedate color. Or perhaps my dramatical sensibilities had been activated by Phoebe and her underlings. In any case, I splurged and had it rutched round the hem, with ribbons to set off the rutchings. How it was ever to be paid for was still a mystery to me.

Perdita's comment that we "would decide on others when you return" made me realize she was toying with the notion of extending our visit.

As her guests had to dine in their afternoon gowns, Mrs. Alton elected to wear her dressing gown to the table. Only John sat down in proper style. He looked handsome and urbane in his black jacket, but the clothing most assuredly did not make the man.

"So what is all this faradiddle about a traveling theater?" he asked me in a quiet aside over dinner, while the other ladies discussed plays and gossip.

I filled him in on our adventure, while he turned several shades paler, and I did not tell him the whole, either. There was no mention of Perdita actually singing for her supper, or myself stealing and receiving shameful propositions. "Good God, if word of this ever gets out, she would be finished before she started. London would be convulsed for a fortnight. Who the devil was this Mr. Brown fellow who was chasing after her? Ought to have his daylights darkened."

"We could not discover his real name. His friend called him Storn, on that first night he showed up. I believe Stornaway was the name of his mother's home, if I recall aright."

"Surely to God she hasn't attached Stornaway!

82

No, it could not be, though your description sounds marvelous like him."

"Why could it not be he, then? And who is he?"

"Worst rake in London."

"That's him."

"Thing is, he is on the verge of an engagement with Lady Dulcinea something or other."

"There was mention of a Dulcinea," I said, harking back to our first encounter again. "That was the name his friend mentioned. The other fellow was called Staff, a nickname obviously."

"Stafford. Yes, it was Stornaway right enough. Confirms it. Tom and Jerry they are called locally, after Cruikshank's cartoons, you know. A pair of young bloods, prime for any sport that offers, though I must own I never heard of him trying to seduce a *lady* before. A *young* lady, I mean, like Perdie."

"They did not know she was a lady."

"Lord no, how should they, and the pair of you rattling through the countryside in company with . . ." He stopped suddenly. "At least they ain't in town," he said, in a more cheerful mood. "Haven't seen nor heard of 'em, and you would if they was here. I'll whistle you two off to Brighton day after tomorrow."

"I don't suppose we could go tomorrow?" I asked hopefully.

"Out of the question. I have a dozen things lined up, but I'll spare an hour to take you for a drive in the afternoon. Wouldn't do me a bit of harm to be seen with a decent looking girl like Perdie. Would please Mama. I don't want the silly chit taking the notion she has attached me, mind."

"You don't have to worry about that," I told him, with a look down the table to her place. As she had not spared him a single glance in a quarter of an hour, it did not seem possible this notion was in her mind.

"Shall we have a few hands of cards to pass the

evening, ma'am?" Perdita asked her hostess when dinner was through.

"Delightful," Mrs. Alton answered, while I examined her for possible contamination. I disliked to be so close to her during her illness, but I believe she was recuperating and was, hopefully, no longer in danger.

The cards were no sooner dealt than there was a hammering at the front door. "I cannot be seen like this!" Mrs. Alton exclaimed, jumping up. She made a hurried exit by the back door of the yellow saloon. Perdita and I were not far behind her. Wearing our afternoon gowns for evening was not our reason for leaving. There was an arrogant sound to that knock that set my hair on end. I had a premonition it would be Lord Stornaway who sought entrance. To verify it, I hid behind the door, while Perdita and Mrs. Alton darted upstairs.

Lord Stornaway was alone. His friend, Stafford, was left out of this visit. "Evening, sir," John said, his face as red as a beet. I got a narrow view of them as the guest was shown in.

"I am Lord Stornaway. You, if my information is accurate, are Mr. Alton," the caller said, in a bold, clipped way.

"That's right. Will you have a seat, milord?"

"No. What I have to say and do won't take long. I want April."

"What? Who?"

"April Spring, the singer from Tuck's."

"I don't know what you are talking about," John said, in true confusion, for I had not told him our second names, nor that Perdita had actually been on the stage. The name of Tuck would alert him to danger, however.

"You had best reconsider your answer, Mr. Alton. The wench is mine, bought and paid for. Daugherty told me she is with you. Produce her, before I am forced to resort to physical persuasion."

"There is nobody here but my mother. She's sick."

"I did not expect you were harboring a pair of lightskirts under your family roof. Where are you boarding them, the girl and her dragon?"

"I don't know what you're . . ."

"Yes, you do. You picked them up at Mother Gaines's place. You drove them away. You have not had time to take them to the country. Logic leads to the conclusion you have got them in a city apartment. You had better give me the address . . ."

"There is some mistake. There is nobody here but my mother and myself. Folker!" he called to the butler, in a quavering voice. My own knees were rattling so hard I feared they would betray my presence.

Folker entered and said in a dignified voice that Mrs. Alton had particularly requested silence, in her condition . . . The ominous words made her condition sound a good deal more serious than it was. "A sick mother does not preclude your having the women under your protection," Stornaway pointed out.

"I tell you they ain't. You have got the wrong bird. It is *Harry* Alton this fellow meant, likely as not," John told him, with an admirable flare for deceit. I had not looked for such wiliness from him.

"That is possible," Stornaway confessed mildly. "I have yet to call on the other Mr. Alton. I have discovered there are two bucks by the name. It is possible they are *both* unlicked cubs in poorly-cut jackets, as Daugherty described the thief."

"Now see here!" John blustered.

"Yes, that is where I *am* seeing. If you have lied to me, Alton, I shall return and peel the hide from your body."

The menacing tone sent my poor heart quivering. I was certain John would give way, but it was nothing of the sort. He prided himself on his "pops," as he termed his fists. "Be very happy to have Jackson set up a match," he answered bravely.

"I look forward to the exquisite pleasure of teaching you a lesson in civility, sir. After I have drawn your cork and let the air out of your gas bag, I shall see you are struck from the list of the Four Horse Club. Good evening, sir. You will be hearing from me again. If I am mistaken, I shall tender you an apology, and if I am not . . ." He laughed a mirthless, evil, ominous laugh, then turned and left the room.

"My condolences to Mrs. Alton on her illness. I hope she makes a speedy recovery," he said in a very civil way to the *butler*.

"Now see what a pickle you have got me in!" John exclaimed, turning to vent his wrath on me, as soon as I appeared from behind the door. "What did he mean about April Spring? I hope it is not *Perdita* he was talking about."

"Yes, it was."

"If that girl gets me barred from the Four Horse Club, I'll . . . I'll . . . Oh, *damme,* Moira, why couldn't you take decent care of her? It was *your* job."

"So many things happened. And really, you know, it is her papa who is trying to ram Mr. Croft down her throat."

"Curst loose screw. Ought to be in Bedlam."

There was a note of pity creeping into his voice as he looked at me. "You realize I cannot take the two of you out driving *now*. If Stornaway ever finds out it is me and not Cousin Harry, I am done for. Finished. *Kaput.* Reputation won't be worth a brass farthing. Devil of a temper. Rules society with an iron thumb."

"He sounds a dangerous character."

"Worst rake in London. Don't know how the deuce you and Perdie ever got mixed up with his likes. Thing to do, I think, just go about my business tomorrow as if nothing was the matter. Go to Jackson's, go on the strut on Bond Street, visit a rout or two in the evening, then next morning the three of us whistle out of here at the crack of dawn. No danger of Stornaway turning up at Grifford's. As well as engaged to Lady Dulcinea. Won't be throwing his cap at Grifford's chit, thank God."

"Who is this Lady Dulcinea you speak of, the one he is engaged to."

"A duke's daughter. Great thundering bore of a girl. Niece of an archbishop, cousin to half the Cabinet members, a stick and a prude."

"How does a man like that come to be dangling after this piece of propriety?"

"Damned if I know. Opposites attract, they say. She'd turn him off in the squeezing of a lemon if she knew how he was carrying on. Keeps all his petticoat dealings on the sly. The ladies don't realize what a wretch he is, and the papas don't care. Got money coming out his ears. Very eligible *parti*. To tell the truth, Moira, there ain't such a thing as a *good* nobleman. All you read of them in the journals is debts and duels. Shabby lot."

"What do you think he will do?"

"Call on Cousin Harry, then come rattling back here when he finds out he's made a mistake. Peel my hide, tan it. I don't mind *that*, but if he blackballs me with the FHC, I will have Perdie killed and stuffed, and you, too."

After this grim speech, he put his head back and laughed, with a light dancing in his dark eyes. "By Jove, he won't, though. Find out, I mean. Cousin Harry went off to Newmarket to put Gretchen through her paces. He is running her in the Two Thousand Guineas. A dashed spavin-backed jade whose only qualification is that she is a three-year old. She won't even go the mile, but Harry don't know a mule from a mare. He left this afternoon. Stornaway will learn he has gone, and think Perdie is with him. By God, I think we will rub through after all, Moira. You will be safe at Aunt Maude's before he gets back from Newmarket, and I'll deny I ever heard of April Spring. How did Perdie disport herself on the stage?" was his next cheerful question.

"Shamefully."

"Wish I had seen her. She is up to anything, but she has a voice like a cat in labor. How did she convince this Daugherty fellow she was a singer?"

"He forgot to listen. Like all the other men, he was too busy looking."

"Getting his eyes full, too, if I know anything. I must have her sing for me sometime. I'll go up and say good night to Mama. I am off to have a few heavy wets with the fellows. Don't wait up for me."

"I was not planning to. I am very tired."

"You look like death warmed over. Better get to bed, my dear. The hoyden will run you a merry chase tomorrow. Tell me, Moira, did *you* sing, too?"

"No, I cooked for the troupe," I told him. He took it for an excellent jest."

I went up to Perdita, who sat smiling at herself in the mirror. "It was Mr. Brown," she said smugly. As if I didn't know! "Was he after me?"

"Yes, he was. Poor John is in trouble with him. Of course he denied knowing a thing about us. We cannot be seen with him tomorrow after all. We won't be able to have our drive."

"You mean we won't be able to drive with John, Moira. I am sure Mrs. Alton will be happy to lend us her carriage. She won't need it, since she is ill. We shall have our drive, never fear."

As the probability was that Lord Stornaway would be chasing off to Newmarket, I felt we might have a brief respite in a closed carriage. One can hardly incarcerate a girl like Perdita. She would only climb out a window and go straggling down Bond Street alone.

"I suppose there is no harm in that."

Then I went to bed and prayed for rain.

Chapter Eight

God was not listening to my prayers. The morning dawned fair and warm. It was all I could do to keep Perdita home till after luncheon. We did not see a sign of John all day. Despite his late carousing, he was up and gone from the house before we came downstairs. He had to crowd a whole year's social activities into six weeks. It was not necessary to ask Mrs. Alton for the loan of her carriage. She offered it. We had no fear of encountering Lord Stornaway poring over the gloves and stockings and fans at the Pantheon Bazaar, and that was where we spent our afternoon. Mrs. Alton had forwarded some large but unspecified sum to Perdita, every penny of which she had to spend. She bought paste buckles for slippers, kid gloves, ribbons, sugarplums, anything that fell under her eyes. I spotted Phoebe, bent on an errand similar to our own. It was feathers that occupied her interest. Jostling about the countryside was hard on her three plumes.

"Well if it ain't Miss High-and-Mighty!" she declared in a loud, vulgar voice when she saw us. "I see your new patron has come down heavy," she went on, casting a jealous eye on our footman, whose arms were laden with our purchases. "Who is he, eh?"

"Lord Stornaway," Perdita told her, with a spiteful little smile.

"I knew it! I can spot a lord a room away. Listen, dear, he had a friend with him the first time. You remember that dark-haired fellow, heavyset, that was dangling after me?"

"Mr. Stafford," Perdita admitted, enjoying the game of teasing her old rival.

"Is that his handle? If you happen to bump into him, you might let him know I am at liberty. You know where I'm putting up."

"Did the interview at the Garden not go well, Phoebe?" I asked.

Remembering her proud boast of the day before, she immediately tried to cover her gaffe. "The deal is pending," she said grandly. "It never does no harm to have another egg in your basket. They want an ingenew, but I feel my talents lay elsewheres. When a lady reaches her mid-twenties, she wants to go on to other parts. That trollop of a Polly is casting sheep's eyes at Mick, trying to con him into letting her play Miranda in our new play coming up. We done it a few seasons ago. I'll not play second lead to no female, and so I told Mick. Would yez like to stop off for a cup of tea, girls?"

A small crowd was beginning to gather around us. There was that in Phoebe—the loud voice, the sable wrap and ostrich plumes—that attracted attention, offstage or on. I was not eager to continue in her company.

"We have to leave now," I told her.

"Lord Stornaway is so jealous if I am gone long," Perdita added mischievously.

"You've ended up in the honeypot for sure," Phoebe said wistfully. "Remember what I said about Mr. Stafford."

"I'll remember," Perdita told her, then the two of

90

us hastened off, while the footman stood behind, smiling after Phoebe's retreating form, till we had to call him to attention.

"There's a fine figure of a woman," he said.

Perdita examined him with some interest, but in the end shook her head, withholding the address. The great Phoebe was not ready to settle for a footman yet.

The remainder of the afternoon passed pleasantly with a drive through Hyde Park, and later admiring our shopping after we got back to Alton's. The modiste arrived to present our gowns to us. Perdita looked every bit as overdressed as I feared she would in her heavily trimmed gown, while my own was cut lower in front than I had intended. I feared Aunt Maude would be scandalized with it, but Mrs. Alton found it "quite dashing," while John was kind enough to inquire if I was setting up in competition with Perdie, at *my* age.

I sat in some trepidation of another visit from Lord Stornaway, but he did not call. After dinner, John deserted us again for the haunts of London bachelors. I was happy our adventure was coming to a close. It would be good to get to Brighton, and turn Perdita over to her aunt. Maude Cosgrove had some influence with Brodie. She would bend his ear, make him send Perdita to her. As a widow, and the girl's maternal aunt, she had always taken a strong interest in her. She might even give her a Season in London. In my own mind, I saw a year from the present as the proper time. Eighteen was a good age to make one's bows, and a year in the life of such a busy womanizer as Stornaway would be long enough for him to forget April Spring. Even if he discerned a resemblance to her in Perdita, he could not be sure. To have her make her bows from such an unexceptionable home as Mrs. Cosgrove's must convince him he was mistaken.

I am so utterly philanthropic as to have forgotten

91

myself in this rosy future. Miss Moira Greenwood, too, must have a roof over her head. I could hardly expect to be presented at St. James's at my advanced years, a quarter of a century in my dish. How had I got so awfully *old* all of a sudden? It seemed I had gone to bed young one night, and awoken old in the morning. It was during my three-year interval of looking after Perdita that the thing had happened. Advancing age was not my only problem, either. The lack of a portion must always be an impediment to a female. In truth, it was this rather than my age that was the more serious blight on my chances. Gentlemen had been known to smile at maturity before now, when it was a golden maturity.

My hope was to be taken into Mrs. Cosgrove's establishment as a part-time chaperone for Perdita, and a part-time companion for Maude. When Perdita was bounced off, which would not take a week if I knew anything, I might grow into a full-time companion for my cousin. She had asked me to her when my mother died, which was the reason for my optimism in this scheme. I would have gone, too, had it not been for Perdita requiring a governess. It had not slipped my mind that the last cousin to find a berth with Mrs. Cosgrove had won a husband. He was a widower, but we poor relations are not so romantic as to require better than a second-hand male to satisfy us. A widower would do very well for me, and as Maude was active socially, it did not seem out of the question.

"We had best turn in," I suggested, as the hands of the clock showed a quarter of eleven. "Mrs. Alton is still recuperating, and John wants to get an early start tomorrow."

"So you are off to Brighton, eh, girls?" Mrs. Alton confirmed. "That's nice. You are close enough that John can visit you from time to time. You must come and spend a week with me later on, when I am back on my legs. In fact, pray consider this house your little *pied-à-terre* in London."

"We shall make our adieux and tender our thanks now, Mrs. Alton, to prevent your getting up early with us in the morning," I said.

"Let Perdita go off without saying good bye? Nothing of the sort!" she insisted.

So our adieux and our thanks were postponed indefinitely. She was not up with us in the morning. John had us called at six. Before seven, we were on the road to Brighton. Anything seems possible on a bright, spring morning. There was some delightful promise in the air, some excitement, to be hurtling along at a rapid pace, with the breeze fanning our cheeks, in the midst of heavy traffic. Even at that early hour the road was well traveled.

"Twenty-eight stagecoaches a day," John informed us, as proud as though he drove every one of them himself. "Busiest turnpike in the country. If you can drive this road, you can drive anything. Prinney is said to have made the trip from his Pavilion to London in four and a half hours, but I for one don't believe a word of it. Besides, he made three stops, and used three nags, harnessed random-tandem. I shan't make but two. We can certainly go farther than Croydon with this pair of steppers I have got, though I shan't push 'em all the way to Horley."

Already at Croydon the team had slowed noticeably, so he changed his mind. "The Prince certainly did not have to wait half an hour for them to change his cattle," he fumed, after we had waited perhaps five minutes for the stableboys to attend us.

At Horley, they were faster. "Wouldn't you *know* when this pest of a girl stops to water herself, they would get us changed in three minutes flat," he grouched. There was a deal more of grouching on the next lap. Not only had they dared to palm a lame jade off on him, but Perdita, accustomed to every

93

luxury, insisted she must stop for something to eat, after having had a drink at Horley.

"Dash it, we might as well have a proper luncheon, or she will want to stop again after half a mile. I don't see why you didn't bring a lunch with you, if you meant to eat every step of the way."

I must say, John ate more than the rest of us, once the stop was actually made. The beefsteak he declared to be "quite tolerable," while the fowl were "decent." An apple tart too was considered "worth eating." This faint praise seemed to be the style with the fashionable bucks this year. With his eyes fairly popping out of his head, he claimed a certain female encountered at the inn door to be "passable." He stopped to have a few words with an acquaintance as we drove back onto the road, dense with traffic now. The friend said, in no low tone, that his friend was "not unattractive," and he would not resent being presented to her.

"Are you taking her to Grifford's?" he went on to ask.

"Lord no! Do you take me for a Johnnie Raw, to be taking an Incomparable to Bromley Hall, when the whole purpose of the party is to nab a *parti* for Millie? They'd have my eyes gouged out and fed to the hounds."

"I hear Tony Hall has popped the question. Daresay the Griffords are sorry they went to the bother of tossing the do," the young fellow announced, with a sly smile to John.

The effect this speech had on John was remarkable. He had described Millicent Grifford as a squinter and an ugly patch, which hardly indicated an interest in her. These descriptions went beyond faint praise to downright denigration. Why then was he white around the lips, and abusing Tony Hall for a lily-livered mawworm?

On this cheery note, we rolled back on the road. Speed was impossible with the number of carriages wheeling to and fro. It was quite alarming to see the congestion. One would think every cottager along the way had set up a carriage, and taken it out for a spin.

The afternoon was half gone by the time we reached Brighton. "Where does this Maude woman live?" John demanded, his temper frayed well beyond civility.

"The Steyne. Is it a decent neighborhood?" Perdita asked.

"Yes, by Jove, very decent," he allowed, conferring its new meaning on the word, to judge by his accent. It was much better than decent, as we saw when we reached it. All the crack, with a view even of the Prince Regent's Pavilion glowing in the distance, lending a fairy-tale enchantment to the scene. "She ain't hiring that place at less than thirty guineas a week," he told us. "Must be rich as a nabob."

"She is not hiring it at all. She owns it," Perdita told him. "And when she dies, she is leaving it to *me*. She told Mama so."

In my own view, it was a great pity she was not leaving it to her more needy cousin, Miss Greenwood. Would it not be marvelous to own a house in Brighton? But that is always the way; those who have, keep getting and getting and getting. But Perdita was her niece, while I was a lesser relative.

"Is she, by Jove?" John asked. "Millie Grifford don't own any fine home in Brighton. Much *I* care if she wants to throw herself away on Tony Hall, dashed rattlepate. Told me she didn't care for him above half, and he called *her* an antidote, too. Well she is next door to an ape-leader, if you want the truth. I have half a mind not to go to Bromley Hall at all. What did Huxley say, anyway? Did he say the Griffords had accepted Hall's offer?"

"No, they only said he had made one," I informed him, hoping to improve his mood.

"He's offered for every chit with a penny in her pocket. The Griffords won't have him. Not that *I* care a groat. Serve him well if he got stuck with her. Only offered to spite me."

"You would not want to marry a *squinter,* John," Perdita pointed out.

"Squinter? Who are you calling a squinter? Millicent makes *you* look like a dashed—well, anyway she don't squint," he decided, after making a mental comparison of the two ladies. I concluded Millicent was a somewhat plain girl, whom John had managed to fall in love with. "And she don't go screeching about on public stages, either. What are you worth in shillings and pence anyway, Perdie? She need not think I mean to cry willow for two seconds, for I don't."

"Plenty, and don't think I would ever marry you, for I would not."

"Your papa will manage to give your blunt to that curst commoner he married. Don't know what he sees in her. Ain't even pretty. Pity he hadn't had the wits to die, before he went soft in the brain."

"Papa is *not* soft in the head."

"A hard heart and a soft head. Whole neighborhood says so. Well, trying to unload you on old Croft. Certainly soft in the head. I say, Perdie, did Croft ever try to make up to you?"

"Yes, he is always telling me I am beautiful."

"No, I mean get his arms around you, and kiss you?"

"Yes, and *that* is when I decided to make a run for it, and why Papa sent me to Aunt Agatha to change my mind, but I cannot believe that even Bath could be as bad as being kissed by Mr. Croft."

John was frowning in a more intense way than usual. I wondered if he was considering offering for her, out of spite and pity, but when he spoke, his true strategy was revealed. "I'll tell you who you would find a capital fellow is Tony Hall," he said.

We dismounted and looked at Mrs. Cosgrove's house. Since the Prince had brought Brighton into fashion, the place had been modernized by having a pair of bows thrown out in front, with a new pediment and columns added on to give it elegance. John stepped up and banged the brass doorknocker. After a suitable wait, he repeated the action. A few minutes later, the door was opened, not by the butler, but by a very junior footman.

"Mrs. Cosgrove ain't home," he told us, then closed the door.

John did not bother knocking this time. He opened the door and barged in. "These ladies are her cousins. They'll wait till she comes. Just as well pleased she ain't here," he explained aside to me. "Means I won't have to step in and do the pretty. I'm late at Grifford's as it is."

"She isn't coming back," the footman said.

"What do you mean, not coming back! Of course she is coming back, cretin," John said angrily.

"Not for a week she ain't. She's gone off to Swindon to visit relatives."

"Swindon! Moira, she has gone home!" Perdita exclaimed, then fell into an unlady-like fit of giggles at the perversity of Fate.

"Has she gone to Sir Wilfrid Brodie's place?" I asked.

"That's it. Are *you* the young lady . . ." he asked, turning to ogle Perdita in open admiration.

"What did she say, exactly?" I asked him.

He examined us in a suspicious manner, then plunged into his story, when Perdita smiled at him. "She got a letter from a Miss Greenwood that the old gaffer was forcing his gel into a match with a manmilliner, and lit out posthaste to rescue the young lady, and bring her here to us. A rare bad skin she was in, hooting and hollering all the morning long."

"She *did* get your letter then, Moira. How nice!" Perdita said. "I knew dear Aunt Maude would not let me down."

I examined the letters unopened on a hall table,

and saw amongst them my last missive from the inn at Chippenham. She had been spared that useless stop at least. "When did she leave?" I asked.

"Five days ago."

"I expect she has gone to Bath by now," I said, thinking aloud. Brodie would not be tardy in getting rid of her. She would go to Bath, learn we were not there, go back to Swindon. The fat was in the fire now! There would be parties out scouring the roads for us.

"What should we do?" I asked John. "We could wait here for her. She will return eventually."

"You can't stay here unchaperoned, in case you-know-who manages to follow your trail. And I ain't about to turn my rig around and go all the way back to London, either. You'll have to come to Grifford's with me for a day or two."

"I cannot like to land in uninvited at a stranger's house party."

"They ain't strangers; they're the Griffords. Know 'em very well. Come along. Dash it, we've wasted I don't know how many hours with this foolishness. Tony Hall will convince 'em I ain't coming. And if she's accepted him, I will tell them I want them to meet my fiancée," he added, with an angry scowl at Perdita.

"No, you must not!" I said hastily. "She doesn't need a broken engagement on top of the rest."

"I am hungry," Perdita said.

"Have you got any food?" John asked the footman.

"Naught but a flitch of bacon and some cheese. I am alone here with my ma. The mistress gave the other servants a holiday to visit relatives. I can boil you a cuppa tea if you like."

"You could cook for us, Moira," Perdita suggested.

"Don't be a sapskull!" John chided, still not believing I had cooked for the actors. "Damme, now she has got *me* hungry. It is always the same. The minute you set foot into a carriage, you get hungry.

We'll try an hotel. With the half of London jauntering here every day, there must be a good dining room."

"It is too early for dinner. Let us have tea," I suggested.

"We cannot end up at Grifford's half an hour into dinner and expect to be fed. We'll eat now. There's no saying we'll find a decent spot between here and Bromley Hall."

We ate dinner at four o'clock, not very long after taking luncheon, then it was back on the road to Grifford's, while John discussed aloud varied and improbable stories to account for taking two uninvited ladies along on what he hoped would be his engagement visit.

Chapter Nine

Bromley Hall lay halfway between Brighton and Eastbourne, on the south coast, just bordering the sea, though the water was not visible from the front of the house. Arriving as we did shortly after the sun had set, very little was visible but for several rectangles of light from the windows, where the lamps within threw some illumination on the ground. I was keenly aware of what a shabby stunt we played on the hostess, arriving with John. Mrs. Grifford was up to it. John's boast that the girl favored him obviously had some truth in it, to judge by the extraordinary kindness we received. I think the family had about given up hope of seeing him.

The dame could not quite hide her surprised chagrin when Perdita first came into the full light, but her words were at least polite. John entered into a jumbled explanation. "I was taking the ladies to visit their aunt at Brighton, but Perdie is such a widgeon she got the dates mixed up. Next week she was supposed to go—her aunt ain't even home. There was nothing for it but to bring them along. I hope you don't mind, Mrs. Grifford."

"I am very happy to have them. What was the name, again?"

"Miss Brodie and Miss Greenwood, her chaperone. Is Tony Hall here?"

"Yes, you will find him in the saloon with Millicent. Which is Miss Greenwood, did you say?"

"The old one."

Mrs. Grifford looked her commiseration at me, at this plain speaking. She took our hands to make us welcome, while John craned his neck towards the saloon. "You are John's cousin, did he say?" she asked Perdita.

"No, just friends," she answered, causing the poor woman to frown in sorrow.

"Neighbors," I threw in, trying to add much more to the word, a suggestion of careless camaraderie that eliminated any romance.

"I don't see Tony," John said, looking back with a worried face.

"Did you want to see him in particular, John? I can send for him, if you like," Mrs. Grifford offered.

"No, what would I want to see that caper merchant for!"

"Millie will want to know you are here. Call Millicent, Tobin," the hostess said to her butler.

A young female came bustling to the hall. Her first welcome was for John. I think she would have been wiser to conceal some of her relief and joy at his arrival. But then, Miss Grifford was obviously not a scheming girl. Neither was she the least bit pretty, though she did not squint. In fact, her eyes were her most pleasing feature, being large and well-fringed. For the rest, she was plain. Plain brown hair, a plain face, a plain figure, a little on the dumpy side. Her best years, too, had passed her by. She was younger than myself, but not by much.

"I was so afraid you weren't coming," she told him frankly. "I thought you must have changed your mind." When she got around to looking at Perdita, she said, "Oh, dear!" in downright harried tones.

Her mother made the introductions. "John never mentioned you, Miss Brodie," she said, crestfallen.

" 'Course I did. I have told you a dozen times about Perdita. Lives a stone's throw from me, back home."

"Are you Perdie?" she asked, blinking. I cannot imagine what John had told her, but certainly he had omitted the fact that the neighbor was outstandingly beautiful.

"He never mentioned you either," was Miss Brodie's ambiguous reply.

A gentleman peered his head around the archway into the hall, his eyes brightly curious. John glanced at him, and pokered up like a ramrod. "I neglected to offer my congratulations on your betrothal, Millicent," he said, in a hearty way, as though it were a matter of infinite indifference to him in any personal way. "Hear you have accepted an offer from Hall. I'm sure I hope you'll both be very happy."

"Tony Hall?" she asked, blinking. "Oh, no! Where did you hear such a thing?"

"Why they are shouting it from the street corners in Brighton, and along the road. Huxley told me. When are the two of you to tie the knot?"

"I have not accepted any offer. I cannot imagine where Huxley heard it."

"Did he *ask?*"

"He—he *did* mention something to Papa, I believe, but—oh, I am not *engaged,* John!"

"Knew it was all a fudge. Huxley has never got a story straight in his life. Well, shall we step in and say how do you do to Tony and the others?"

"Why do you not take the girls up and show them a room first, Millicent?" her mother suggested. There was some meaningful look on the mother's face, conveying, I suspect, a command to discover what she could of the relationship between the neighbors.

"We have neighbors coming in for a party, ladies,"

she continued. "You will want to change, and make your preparations."

"I'll just toddle on and make myself at home. Ah, there is Hall, hiding behind the doorjamb like a monkey. I say, old chap . . ." He was off, beaming from ear to ear, to roast Tony Hall about the refused offer.

Millicent took us above, up a stately set of broad oaken stairs, to a wide hallway with two dozen doorways opening off it. We were shown into rooms standing side by side. She left Perdita off first, then took me on to my room.

"Miss Brodie is very pretty, is she not?" she asked. "I cannot think why John never mentioned it."

"He does not realize it. You know how it is when people grow up next door to each other. They never think of appearance. Why, they are practically like brother and sister."

"Brother and sister?" she asked hopefully.

"Yes, good friends, in a purely platonic way," I assured her, making the statement freely, to save her the shame of drawing it out of me. I felt, too, our welcome would be warmer if this fact were established. "John was very worried about Tony Hall," I added, to clinch our acceptance.

"He need not have been. He is not at all . . . not that I mean to disparage him, you know, it is only that . . ."

"Yes, I understand." He did not appear very different from John, only fairer of complexion. What magical element was it that caused the strange attraction we call love? And why did it forever go on eluding *me*?

Miss Grifford pointed out the conveniences of the room, expressed her pleasure at seeing us, and concern at our having missed our aunt at Brighton.

"Such a stupid mistake really," I said. "But we shan't billet ourselves on you for long. We can return to London tomorrow." Actually I was not sure

John would take us, nor that the Griffords would be happy to lose him so soon, either.

"I hope you will stay longer than that!" she said, quite warmly, then she fled back downstairs to find John.

I was coming to see that we must notify someone of our whereabouts. I was consulting with myself on the advisability of writing home to Sir Wilfrid versus writing to Aunt Maude. I preferred the latter, but knew not where to post a letter. I should have left word at Brighton of our new destination.

As soon as she saw Millie pass by the door, Perdita came in to join me. "Is she not an ugly squab?" she asked.

"About the same size as yourself—perhaps a few inches taller."

"I cannot fancy John ever offering for her."

"She seems very nice. How do you think I should let Aunt Maude know we are here, Perdita?"

"Write and tell her," she answered simply.

"Yes, my dear, but write *where?*"

"You will know what it is best to do," she said airily. Her present interest was to devise a coiffure that would cast the ladies belowstairs into the shade. While she discussed this with herself, I sat down to dash a quick note off to Mrs. Cosgrove, at all the possible places she could be. Bath, Swindon and Brighton must each have a message awaiting her. She would surely turn up at one or the other of them before long. I was still at this chore when our pitiful bit of baggage was brought up. One small case held our one decent evening dress each, and the nightgown and linens borrowed from Mrs. Alton, along with Perdita's foolish purchases from the Pantheon Bazaar.

Perdita hung up our gowns, while I finished the letters. Then I indulged her in the wish for a new hairstyle, one seen on the streets of London, but that did not suit her in the least. Her hair had not been up in papers the night before, and lacked a curl. This being the case, it looked better pinned up, though the older style was not the optimum one for her face. It made her look a little like a child aping her elders. Neither was the hastily ordered gown ideal for a *young* lady. The bows were too numerous and too dazzling a shade of pink, close to red. I was not entirely pleased with my own gown, either, though it was attractive enough. Normally I would have worn a scarf around the neck, or at least a piece of lace tucked in at the front, for Miss McGavin had really cut it a good inch lower than I liked.

With so few accessories on hand, I was obliged to go belowstairs as I was, and maintain a rigidly erect posture, for propriety's sake, assuring myself a small country party was not crucial for us. The guests were arriving in two's and three's when we descended to the hallway. They were of the very primmest. The vicar's son and daughter came in, the girl wearing a gown cut up to her clavicle. She was amazed to see bare arms on the two of us. She actually bit her lower lip in astonishment, and turned a startled countenance on her brother.

She was followed by a squire's brood, two girls and two young men. Perdita alone exposed more flesh then the two girls together. "You had better run up and get that shawl you bought at the Bazaar," I said to her. It was, unfortunately, a shade of robin's egg blue that would clash hideously with either her outfit or my own, but jarring colors were coming to seem preferable to flesh tones.

John came sauntering out to the hall as we prepared to make our grand entrance. "Well, Perdie, don't you look fine as ninepence," he congratulated, ogling her shoulders. "You don't wear that sort of a getup when you are at home, by the living jingo. Very nice. You will make Mil—the other ladies sit up and take notice. You don't look as dowdy as usual either, Moira. Must be the provincial company throws

106

the two of you into a fashionable light. A rum do," he cautioned. He was being cosmopolitan, to repay Millicent for scaring him. Now that he knew she still cared for him, he would mete out his revenge. But really he was as merry as a grig, beneath his condescension. "Two of the girls squint like a barrel of nails, and t'other is a squealer for looks. Of course they scraped the bottom of the bucket to find the ugliest ones they could, to make Millie look well. Better lookers might show up later. They are just beginning to come in. Tony says they are threatening a game of all fours, but Mrs. Grifford has promised some dancing later on. He says they have been in a pelter all day looking out for my carriage. Can't imagine why."

He latched his arm through ours as he spoke, to lead us in to meet the much maligned company. There was another knock at the door as we turned to leave. He looked over his shoulder to appraise whatever female entered. There was a muffled wheeze deep in his throat, followed by a crippling pressure on our arms. Before I could see what had come in, he tore into the saloon.

"What is it, John?" I asked. Oh, but I knew! I knew before I finished the question who had come in. Who else but our old nemesis could have affected him so deeply?

"I'm done for. It's Stornaway!"

Perdita coo'd in pleasure, unlatched her fingers from John's arm, and turned to leave us. I tightened my hold, and expect John did the same, as she emitted a little scream.

Chapter Ten

Stornaway was detained a few moments in the hallway with the hostess, presumably making some explanation for his precipitate entrance at her party, uninvited. "He *can't* be here! He wouldn't know Millicent from Adam," John protested futilely. "I made sure I was safe once I got inside . . . He cannot be *staying*. He has come to the door asking for directions, just to get a peek and see if we are here. Some of my friends must have tipped him the clue I was coming. That flap-jawed Huxley is out causing mischief again. Never gets anything straight."

"He got this straight at least," Perdita said happily.

Despite John's harried protests of impossibility, it was soon known in the saloon that Lord Stornaway was here, and was to remain, at least overnight. Our informant was Miss Grifford, her face white with astonishment. "Lord Stornaway has come," she said. "His carriage has lost a wheel just in front of our place, and he came to ask if he might stable it, and cadge a drive to the nearest inn, so Mama invited him to remain overnight. She is acquainted with his mama, you see, and once he learned *you* are here,

John, he accepted an offer to join our party tonight. I did not know he was a friend of yours."

"We rattle around town together a bit," he informed her, not slow to claim friendship when it was clear as a candle Millicent was vastly impressed.

"Is he just staying tonight?" I asked, hope rising. We could stave him off for one evening.

"He only mentioned tonight, but Mama hopes she might induce him to remain longer."

One could almost hear the mama's mental gears ground round. Get Stornaway to stay and divert Perdita's interest, so that John might be free to fall in love with Millicent. I acquit her of planning to nab Stornaway for her own daughter. She was too sensible a dame to harbor that scheme. It was impossible to discuss our maneuvers in front of Millicent. The whole had to be arranged by thought transfer, by reading between the lines, and by minute raisings of the brow or lip. My own notion was that there was safety in numbers. If we ensconced ourselves in the midst of a large group, he would not be likely to stalk forward and accuse us publicly of our crimes. Even a Stornaway must have *some* circumspection.

With this end in view, I hinted Millicent into presenting her party to us. There was no difficulty in getting the provincial beaux to clump around Perdita. By a judicious sprinkling of comments and compliments, I installed myself in the midst of the vicar's and squire's daughters.

That is how Stornaway found us, when he entered the saloon some quarter of an hour later. With a truly single-minded purpose, he advanced to Perdita, who turned to greet him, her eyes dancing with laughter.

"Lord Stornaway, what a pleasant surprise!" she said, with a bold smile.

"Hallo, April," he answered. "I did not think you would be surprised to see me. I warned Mr. Alton of

110

my intentions. Come and tell what you have been up to these few days since I have seen you." He held out his hand; she took it, and arose. That easily, he cut her apart from her safe numbers of admirers.

As he led her to a private sofa, he cast one scathing, triumphant, menacing glare at me. "How is business, Molly?" he asked.

"Good evening, Lord Stornaway. Nice to see you again. Did you enjoy Newmarket?" I asked.

"I did not go to Newmarket, ma'am. I felt the more interesting race was being run from London. At least the filly I am interested in ran from London."

"I don't think you are wise to pursue that one."

"Your advice comes too late. I have already bought her." On this meaningful phrase, he proceeded towards the sofa in the corner. I could not like to see him alone with Perdita, but as long as they remained in the crowded saloon, and did not make any public exhibition, I would tolerate it, though every fiber of my being longed to dash over and pull her away by main force. I would have had to do just that to extricate her, for the silly, bold chit was flirting a mile a minute with him.

The good country folks present were not accustomed to such a brazen display of coquetry. She tossed her head, rolled her eyes, made mouths, primped her hair and smoothed her skirts in an endless display of bad manners. Every trick she had picked up from the forward actresses was put into execution, while Stornaway sat back, inciting her to ever greater lengths of vulgarity by his approval. As her laughter rose to immoderate heights, and as Mrs. Grifford began to look more frequently to the corner, I could stand it no longer. I arose and joined them.

"Try and remember where you are, and what you are, Perdita, and act like a lady," I said angrily.

"Now you have just been telling me that is your special line, April, *acting* like a lady. Do as your

111

mentor tells you. Let me see whether I can pass you off as a polite mistress, or must consign you to your apartment," said Stornaway.

I had chosen my words ill, to have mentioned acting. His reply revealed that Perdita was making a game of the occasion, going along with his misconception. She was not really a bad girl, only young, innocent and ignorant as a lamb of such a character as Stornaway. In her mind, I knew she saw herself as the leading character in some romantic comedy. Every gesture was recognized from the mirror academy.

"I should think out of respect for your hostess you would choose some other time and place for this display of bad manners, milord," I was goaded into retorting.

"Well acted, Molly. You have worked in some lady's household in your salad days, if I am not mistaken. That sharp ear of yours has picked up the intonations of gentility very well. You must try if you cannot pass them along to your charge. Would you care to suggest another time and place for our meeting? Say your room, around midnight?"

Perdita lifted her fingers to her mouth and snickered into them, while I scolded her severly. Mrs. Grifford came forward and told us there was some dancing about to begin in another room. I did not know wether to welcome the news or not, but when Perdita bounced up immediately, ready to abandon Stornaway, I quickly decided it was good. He turned to follow her, but I detained him by a fast hand on the arm. He raised an imperious brow, ready to physically shake me off. I longed to slap that lean, arrogant, aristocratic face.

"I would like this opportunity to speak to you in private a moment," I said, very firmly. With Mrs. Grifford looking on, her eyes as big as apples, he did not argue, but sat down impatiently.

"Well, well," he said, leaning back to make himself comfortable. "Fancy meeting you here, Molly. I made sure Alton's first move would be to consign you to Jericho. It will be mine. What's a girl like you doing in a nice place like this, if I may rearrange an old cliché? Is this in the nature of a dress rehearsal for April's debut at the Garden, or do you plan to present her as St. James's instead? She made some comical sounds about being a real lady, when first I joined her."

"What are you doing here?"

"I asked you first, and am still awaiting an answer. Well?"

"We are visiting friends."

"Friends who never heard of you, till Alton had the impertinence to drag you in, uninvited."

"Why did you come?"

"*I* am visiting friends. But mostly I have come to collect my filly."

"I don't know what you are talking about."

"Our three-cornered deal with Daugherty. He was to give you your cut, fifty-fifty, right down the middle. I went back and beat my five hundred out of him, for letting her bolt."

"Five hundred! He told me fifty!"

"Ah, the subject *did* arise, did it? How fallible a thing is woman's memory. A little more assistance and you might remember which stocking top you have your share tucked into. I mean to have April, or my money back."

"I didn't take a single sou from him. I had no idea what he was up to."

"Tch, tch. What a lying rogue it is! You're a sly one, Molly, and a better actress than April will ever be, but you are no match for me. If you are wise, you will stand aside and let me through. I am not about to be bested by a female of your ilk. I cut my teeth several years ago, where bawds are concerned."

"I don't have the money, I tell you."

"I don't want the money. I want April. What did you do with so much blunt? I see April is decked in new silk and too many yards of gaudy ribbon. A new costume yourself as well, if I am not mistaken?" he added, subjecting my body to a bold scrutiny.

"They weren't bought with *your* money."

"I am perfectly sure you talked that greenhead of an Alton into footing your recent bills. Really, the outfit on April . . ." He shook his head in consternation.

"If I could get five hundred pounds, would you leave?" I asked. It was coming to seem five hundred pounds was not too steep a price to pay to be rid of this persistent rake. Had I had such a sum in my possession, I would have given it to him, but of course I had not. "Perhaps John can arrange something."

"*John,* is it? Very chummy. I am somewhat confused about the relationship existing between the three of you. Is it possible he is *your* lover? He don't seem jealous enough of April to be hers."

"Jealous? Of course he is not jealous! He came here to offer for Miss Grifford. And he is not my lover, either; he is only a greenhead of a boy."

He looked unconvinced. "True, but some greenheads prefer older women. You are hardly long in the tooth yet. I am surprised you have forsaken your prime calling so early in life. I assume you started out like April."

"Assumptions like that about a decent woman can get you into a deal of trouble, sir. If you don't stop pestering us, I'll . . ."

His lips stretched into a slow, lazy smile. "I am perched on the edge of my chair. What dire fate impends?"

"I would like to whip you."

"I am not much given to violence myself. I leave it to the lower orders. Nor do I like shows of ill-bred manners in polite company, either. We shall talk again, *very* soon, *very* privately, Molly. I am off to join the dancers. I hear a fiddle scraping, and the

114

hammering of an out-of-tune pianoforte. It must quite take you back to Tuck's. Is April to perform for the company tonight?"

I was too overwrought to reply to this taunt. I let him go to the dancing room, though I intended following very soon. A local fellow, Mr. Leveson, came forward and asked me if I would care to dance, giving me an excellent opportunity to do so.

There was a country dance forming lines down the two sides of a room that was too small to hold the party properly. John stood at the head with Millicent Grifford opposite him. Halfway down was Perdita with one of the squire's sons, the handsomer one. Stornaway was leading the squire's daughter into the set, and I stood at the end with my partner. Leveson was a mature, sensible-seeming man of provincial accent, but good manners.

I enjoyed the remainder of the evening about as much as anyone enjoys a visit to the tooth drawer. Perdita behaved in a rowdy, loud fashion she had never followed at home. I don't know whether it was her being amongst strangers that accounted for it, or her recent experience with the actresses, or whether Stornaway in some inexplicable way goaded her on. I know he was at her side as often as he could be, and she was worse when she was with him. He fed her a good deal of wine too, more than she was accustomed to. Over all, I suppose it was having a whole bunch of gentlemen to lord it over that set her up in her own conceit, that and the absence of her father, who could always tame her with a single glance.

On top of worrying about her making a show of herself, I kept a sharp eye peeled to see if Stornaway accosted John, whom he certainly watched like a hawk, as I did myself. I used the excuse of a waltz to have some privacy with John.

"Damme, I don't want to waltz with you, Moira! Millicent won't be jealous of an old crow like you."

115

"Never mind that. We must talk. Has Stornaway said anything to you?"

"Yes, he asked me if I had given up all thoughts of being a member of the FHC, after being rigged out with the outfit," he answered with a dismal frown. "He is going to have me kicked out, and it is all Perdie's fault. I *told* him I ain't a bit interested in her, and the cretin took into his head I favor *you*. Begins to look as though the fellow has a couple of tiles loose. He wants to talk to me tonight, in my room."

"He might ask you for five hundred pounds. I don't suppose you happen to have five hundred you could spare, John? I begin to think it is the easiest way to be rid of him."

"Yes, the easiest way for *you!* Where the deuce would I get a monkey? Can't ask Papa for it. Already let me trade my grays in on the bays, and outfitted me for the FHC. I'll never get to wear my striped waistcoat, and the dotted tie."

"We must leave here as soon as possible. Tomorrow morning."

"Dash it, I can't leave tomorrow. It is Millie's birthday. That is what they are using for an excuse for this party, her birthday. They ain't mentioning it's her twenty-third, so don't twit her about it. They don't want to admit she's so ancient. I must stay, and you will have to stay, too, for you can't strike out on the roads alone with Stornaway on the loose. We'll leave the next morning. Tony is leaving then. I'll decide tomorrow whether or not to offer for Millie."

"Are you really thinking of marrying her?"

"What's the matter with her?" he asked, so hotly that I understood it was only pique that Tony had beat him to it that prevented his speaking tonight.

"Nothing. She is very nice. I like her."

"Had the sense to send Tony off with a flea in his silly ear, at least. You'll have to keep a tight rein on Perdie tomorrow, keep her out from under my feet.

116

Millie don't trust her above half. Lord, as though I would ever care for Perdie Brodie, the hussy."

John was certainly enjoying his last evening as a bachelor, or experiencing it; he had little enjoyment, to judge by his frowns. It was a great pity he had to choose this time to become entangled, but that is unfair. The pity was that *we* should have intruded our problems on him at such a time.

A supper was served after the dancing interval. Stornaway was at Perdita's side, with a squire's son at her other side, and equally attentive. John sat with Millicent, while I had the pleasure of Mr. Leveson's escort, which saved me from the ignominy of eating with the oldsters. There was talk of the morrow's activities. The Griffords were having a picnic at the seashore in the afternoon, with a birthday dinner and dance in the evening. I expect their hope was to announce their daughter's engagement as well. As I observed Perdita juggling her two beaux in loud glee, with Stornaway casting furtive and troublesome glances from John to myself between smiles at her, as I considered the rake's firm declaration that he did not mean to leave without either the girl or his money, and that we had not the money, I was in some doubt as to smooth sailing through the next day and evening.

Chapter Eleven

I rather expected to see John come to breakfast the next morning with a black eye, or a bent nose, from Stornaway's threatened late night visit. The reason he did not was soon explained. "With all the extra company landed in on them—you and Perdie and Stornaway—the Griffords asked me to share my room with Tony Hall. They *had* put me in the best guest suite in the place, can't imagine why. Millie was out-of-reason cross when I had to be moved, but a lord after all, they could not stable him with that yahoo of a Tony Hall. Stornaway got my suite. Tony tells me there was a rare dust-up when someone busted into old Mrs. Peachum's room and found her unplugging her false teeth and untying her stays. It was certainly Stornaway, looking for me."

It was delightful to envisage Stornaway pouncing in on an unsuspecting widow, in mid-toilette. Before the image faded from my mind, we had the rake-lord in person to observe. He came to the table at nine o'clock, immaculately garbed, shaved, combed, and so on. His elegance made one acutely aware of the plain provincial jackets of most, and the foppish raiment of the temporary citified bucks such as John. The noble guest made a bow, expressed a few pleasantries about the felicity of the weather remaining good for the planned picnic, then began looking around the table to select a place. He was soon advancing to that end where John and I sat conversing. Alton was not tardy to arise and begin making his excuses to leave.

"I am to meet Millicent for a ride this morning," he mentioned.

"You won't forget to leave a half hour free for *me*, Mr. Alton?" Stornaway asked, in a seemingly polite tone, but when one knew what to look for, the menace beneath was not hard to find.

"Oh, certainly. I want to talk to you again about the FHC."

"I want to talk to you about a different matter. Shall we say—half an hour before luncheon, in the saloon?"

"Fine, I'll be there."

"Don't disappoint me." Then he turned his dark eyes to me. "I hope you slept well, Molly?"

"My name is Miss Greenwood. I slept very well, thank you."

"I am so happy to hear it, Molly. April as well enjoyed a good night's rest? I don't want the girl looking hagged."

"Miss Brodie enjoyed a good night's rest."

"What time can we expect her to arise?"

"She arises when she feels like it. Apparently she does not feel like it yet."

"I can wait. I am taking her for a drive in my curricle this morning."

"The three of us will be squeezed, milord. Don't think you are taking her alone anywhere, for you are not."

"I never object to being squeezed by women. I consider it one of life's little joys." We fell silent while his breakfast was served. When the servant

120

left, he continued. "Alton hid on me last night, making it impossible for me to come to terms with him. But I begin to realize it is yourself who is in charge of business matters for the group. Have you spoken to him?"

"Yes, and he does not have five hundred pounds to spare, so you might as well go away and leave us alone." The table was only half full, but we were sufficiently far away from the others that a private exchange was possible. For some reason, I preferred to hold our discussion within shouting distance of help.

"Recouping my money was really second choice. I would rather have April. In fact, to show my good will in this matter, I am willing to give you Daugherty's portion of the finder's fee as well, the half a thousand pounds I beat out of him. Actually four-fifty; he had spent some. Deliver April to me—say, at the edge of the village this afternoon. I shall leave with her, and you will not be bothered by me again."

"What do you want with her?"

"What do you think?"

"She is only a *child!*"

"I have not the least aversion to youth, provided it is accompanied by beauty. In fact, I am strange enough to prefer it."

"Can you not even *consider* that she might be an innocent girl?"

"I *did* consider it, for all of sixty seconds, ma'am, and decided in the negative. She is so vulgar I question at times whether I even want her, but she is young enough yet to be trained properly. Not to disparage your efforts in that direction. I am sure you have improved her out of all recognition of her origins. It will be for me to apply the finishing luster only. Sharp as you are, Molly, one cannot expect a female of your sort to know the fine details pertaining to passing oneself off as a lady."

"It is truly astonishing to me that a gentleman born into a noble family, with all the advantages of education, wealth, and perhaps even a *little* of native intelligence, should waste his time in such a degrading fashion. Can you find nothing better to do with your time and money than to squander them on the pursuit of fallen women?"

"I have several equally worthy avocations. I gamble, race horses, box, drive up to the bit, dance quite superbly. I shall give you a sample of the last named this evening, if the occasion should arise."

"I shall take very good care that it does not."

"C'est à vous. I speak French too. I must give April lessons."

"I wish you luck of that endeavor."

"What, have you tried?" He set his head back and laughed loud enough that the other heads at the table turned towards us. "Good God, I would like to have seen it; the one-eyed leading the blind. As you are so ambitious for her, you ought really to welcome me, you know. I mean to turn her out in the first style."

"No, milord, in the Stornaway style, which I am convinced is well removed from the first style of anything but dissipation."

"I am not a pervert after all! You won't do better for her than me. I am quite an adept at pleasing a woman. I am not hard to get along with, am generous and considerate."

"A pattern-card of polite behavior. You are ready to do everything for a girl but marry her. Excuse me, for some unaccountable reason, I have lost my appetite, but it would not do to suggest you have turned my stomach, milord."

He arose and helped me from my chair. There was a self-conscious, almost an embarrassed look on his face. "I don't need any help," I said curtly.

"You are singularly able to handle your tongue

certainly, but a *lady* usually accepts assistance in managing her chair. A tip for you, Molly."

I glared hard at him, then strode upstairs to awaken Perdita.

When I went to her room, she was gone. The bed was unmade, had been slept in. Her evening gown was thrown over the dresser. Her pelisse and reticule were missing. She had left, sneaked out. There had been no response when I knocked on her door before going downstairs. Thinking she slept, and that asleep in her bed was the least troublesome place for her, I had not entered. She had not come down while I was at the table. She must have been gone already when I knocked, close to three-quarters of an hour before. I felt a tide of panic well up in me. John—I must see John!

My hope was that he had not yet gone to the stable with Millie. I encountered Mrs. Grifford in the hall belowstairs. "I don't suppose you have seen Miss Brodie?" I asked, trying to keep the excitement from my voice.

"To be sure I saw her before the gentlemen came to pick her up," she answered in a tone of sweet reason.

"Gentlemen?" I trembled inwardly at the awful plural sound of it. How many gentlemen had she set up an assignation with?

"The Manners fellows, Lou and Bob. They are taking her for a spin into the village, Miss Greenwood. You cannot mean she has not your permission? Had I thought it for a moment, I would have had you called."

I hardly knew what reply to make. It was a question of my looking careless, or Perdita dreadfully forward and sly.

My temper was not assuaged in the least when Stornaway, finished with breakfast, came into the hallway. "Yes, of course I knew she was going, but I did not know exactly what the destination was."

"I wager it is Miss Brodie whose destination you are discussing," he said, strolling up to us, with a conning smile levelled on Mrs. Grifford.

"It happens it is," she smiled uneasily, not accustomed to having a rakish lord underfoot, but not quite disliking it, either, I think. "No harm can come to her in the village, and the Manners lads are not likely to misbehave. They are only foolish; there is no vice in them. Millicent has driven out with one or the other of them countless numbers of times."

"Has John left yet?" I asked her, wondering if I could induce him to bring her back. Two foolish young men and one lady totally lacking in propriety might well fall into a muddle, even without any vice being involved.

"Why, Miss Greenwood, you must know *I* am very happy to put my carriage at your disposal," Stornaway offered at once.

"John and Millicent left fifteen minutes ago," she told me, with utter contentment of the fact. "Kind of you to offer your carriage, Lord Stornaway. I cannot think it necessary, but if you want to go after her, Miss Greenwood, there is your answer."

I was obliged to thank him, for the looks of it, though I had a fair idea his carriage did not come without its owner, and going with him was not a part of my plan.

"You are correct. There is no need to go after her. She will be back in an hour," I said firmly.

"I hope you were comfortable last night, Lord Stornaway. May we look forward to the pleasure of your remaining with us a few days?" the hostess said, with an ingratiating smile.

'You are too kind, ma'am. I shall impose on your generosity one day more, if I may? My carriage is repaired, but the company so delightful I am in no hurry to leave."

I went up to my room, to return downstairs by the servants' staircase. I asked a servant to have Mr.

124

Alton's curricle brought round to the front for me. I had never handled a team of high steppers in my life. The family gig, with one sluggish nag, was the extent of my experience as a whip, unless I ought to include my experience with Ginger.

When I went out to the front, the curricle was awaiting me. The groom aided my ascent, handed me the ribbons, and I was off. The famous bays set a fast pace. I always assumed John exaggerated a good deal when he spoke of sixteen miles an hour. From the passenger's seat, it seemed like ten or twelve at the most. I expect it was holding the ribbons that led him astray. The speed was strangely accelerated when it was myself who was expected to lead them. The village, I knew, lay about two miles to the east, but my inexpert yanking at the reins set the animals off in the opposite direction. By drawing hard, I finally got them to stop, but had not a single notion what sign would get them turned around. In desperation, I clambered down from my perch and went to their heads, to try to talk them around.

When I heard horse hooves behind me, I looked in hopes of a rescuer, but what I saw was Lord Stornaway sitting in a racy curricle of his own, wearing a grin that split his face from ear to ear. He had a tiger behind him. He tossed his reins to this boy, before jumping down to assist me. "Out for a pleasure spin, I assume, Molly? I had a strong feeling you would want air."

"That's it, just taking the morning breezes."

"The team are mulish, are they not? Do you think it possible they don't speak English? It is perfectly clear you will not make the village without crippling Alton's team. Much as I dislike the fellow, I could not wish such a fate on him, knowing what an inordinate sum he paid for them. Hop into my rig. I'll take you, while my tiger returns Alton's cart to the stable. I am going to beat you there, in any case. Would you not prefer to be with me when I abduct her?"

125

The face I turned on him must have revealed my terrified feelings. "Don't worry. I do not mean to endanger my own reputation by doing anything so foolish. It will be arranged much more discreetly than by kidnapping. Come along."

A rapid survey of my options inclined me to accept his offer. Certainly he would get there before me, if I ever got there at all, which seemed unlikely, with the team heading in the other direction. I reluctantly climbed into his curricle, while his tiger took control of John's.

"You know, horses are a little like men, Molly," Stornaway began, in an avuncular tone, as we darted towards the village.

"I notice the resemblance," I said, staring fixedly at the horses' posteriors as we progressed.

When he made no reply, I risked a glance at him. He was chewing a smile, trying not to betray any amusement. When his eyes met mine, he gave up chewing and laughed aloud. "Score one for you. What I was about to say was that they are more biddable to reasonable commands than blind force."

"Alton's pair were about as biddable to reason as you are. I have exhausted argument. What have you in mind?"

"Consider the carrot, versus the stick. You use only the latter. You have double-crossed me, and had the temerity to lecture me on morals into the bargain. Now isn't it time we got down to sweet reason? Let me describe my carrot."

"Describe away. I am listening."

"My offer is generous. Your refusing it can only mean you hope for a better one. Why don't you just tell me what your price is, and we can bargain from there."

"That is where reason breaks down, sir. She is not for sale, at any price. This is not a piece of merchandise we are discussing, but a human being."

"I see."

I looked hopefully to see if he did indeed understand, or was only devising some other scheme. "Already sold her to someone else?" he asked bluntly.

"This talk is pointless. If you will let me down in the village, I shall join Perdita and her friends."

"She is not averse to my offers, you know."

"She must misunderstand them."

"I never mentioned the word marriage."

"There are girls, of a type probably unfamiliar to you, to whom the word love implies marriage."

"Not sure I mentioned love, either. But you are mistaken about my unfamiliarity with that type. They are tediously familiar to me."

"You would find any hint that you do the right thing *tedious,* of course," I said, in a dismissing way.

We continued in silence till the village was reached, traversed its length, both looking about for a sign of her. She was not at all difficult to spot. She sauntered down the street between the two bucks picked up the night before, with an ice cone in her fingers, and a kitten tucked into the crook of the other elbow.

"Please draw up here," I asked in a cold but respectful tone.

I was surprised that he obliged me without a word. I hopped down, thanked him, and joined my charge. "See the sweet little kitten Lou gave me," she said, holding it out in one hand, with its feet stroking the empty air. I believe one of its claws must have scratched her. She emitted an unlady-like squeal, and dropped it. I picked it up, and suggested we go home.

"We just got here," she pointed out.

"Where were you before you came here? You left the house hours ago."

"We stopped at a farm to pick up the kitten. I call him Lou, after my friend," she informed me, with a shameless batting of her lashes at Mr. Manners, who smiled fondly. "And Bob is going to get me a puppy," she added, ladling out a smile to her other adorer.

"This is not the time to be picking up a menagerie, Perdita, when we are not quite settled down."

"I miss all my pets at home so. We should have brought some kittens with us."

"Would you please take us home now?" I asked the elder and saner-appearing of the Manners fellows, the one called Bob.

"Where is Stornaway going?" she asked.

"Back to Bromley Hall, I suppose."

"What, and did he offer to take you out for a drive? Was he not coming here to see *me?*"

"He brought me here to collect you," I said in a damping way.

"He might have got down and said good morning. *I* think you are trying to steal him from me."

"You think wrongly. Come along."

"My bonnet. My new bonnet. I cannot leave without it."

"Where did you get the money to buy a bonnet?"

"Bob had to lend me a little. After I told the woman I would take it, I learned I had not quite enough money, but John will pay him. It is only a crown. Would you mind picking it up at the milliner's for me, Bob?"

Bob, with a leery glance at his brother, darted across the street to pick up the bonnet, and soon rejoined us. As the outing was thoroughly ruined with my harping presence, the three agreed to return home very shortly afterwards. The boys let us off at the main entrance. There was a group of young guests playing croquet on the lawn, with another bunch watching them. They made a charming scene, the ladies' colorful gowns appearing like huge flowers against the green of the lawn. I was momentarily entranced with it, till a thorn sprang into view, amidst the flowers. Stornaway was there, advancing towards us.

"Mission accomplished?" he asked. "I made sure it was safe to leave the matter in your capable hands, Molly. I see you have been shopping, April. What did I buy? And here you swore the money was all gone," he said, wagging a finger at me.

"I bought a bonnet," Perdita told him. "And the money *is* all gone. I had to borrow from Bob Manners, but John will pay him back. Would you like to see it?" She handed the kitten to me, took the box, and began untying ribbons, there in the open air, in front of a gathering group. Groups of males tend to gather rather quickly when Perdita appears.

"Later," I said, grabbing her hand and trying to pull her into the house.

"We would all adore to see the bonnet!" Stornaway insisted, egging her on.

"It is *very* dashing. All the crack, like the one Phoebe wore, Moira, with three ostrich plumes, only mine are white."

"I was hoping for red!" Stornaway said, feigning chagrin. "She could not do better than to take Phoebe for a model," he added aside to me, with a hateful grin.

I finally got her away, lecturing her at the top of my bent while she posed in front of the mirror, in the most outrageous bonnet ever seen outside of Tuck's Traveling Theater. The kitten leapt to the bed and began clawing at the counterpane, obliging me to hold it, to save Mrs. Grifford's bedding. Perdita's love of animals did not extend to offering them any care. It was I who had to go to the kitchen begging a saucer of milk, and take Lou outdoors before luncheon. I heartily wished it would find its way back to the farm from whence it had come.

Chapter Twelve

When it was time for the picnic, Perdita remembered Lou, the feline Lou, and made a great show of having everyone look for it. "You have *lost* him, Moira! How *could* you be so cruel, thrusting a poor little kitten outdoors alone?"

"I lost my head," I told her, angry sparks shooting from my eyes, or so I imagined.

Really the girl was becoming impossible. Every foolish gentleman of the party began running around, looking behind bushes and under the verandah for the animal, while Millicent stood with a patient smile, as Perdita took John's hand and led him around to the stable to look. When they had found it and returned, Perdita, with her pet in her arm, walked rather quickly towards John's curricle, despite the fact that she and everyone else knew he had arranged to drive Millicent. The only smile on the lawn was Tony Hall's. Stornaway was there, watching her performance, with an expression that resembled a gathering sneer.

"You might offer her a drive in your rig, as you are

always so eager for her company," I said sharply to him.

"I was hoping for the pleasure of driving *you*, Molly," he replied, still in his sneering way. He walked forward to invite her, however. "Now I am *assured* of your company," he said.

"I will be happy to join you. And you will hold that curst kitten yourself, Perdita."

"Isn't she *mean*, Lord Stornaway? How could anyone find my little Lou-lou a curst kitten? Moira has no way with animals."

"I know she has no love of horses," he agreed.

As Stornaway was looking more at me than herself, Perdita set up a pantomime for his benefit. The kitten was held up, its nose touching her own, while she gurgled and coo'd of her affection for the creature. When she had his attention, she handed it to me, but I steadfastly refused to have my gown destroyed by its claws, and handed it back to her.

The only pleasure of the trip was that the kitten put several snags in Stornaway's jacket before we reached the seaside. Our entertainment during the drive was to hear every vulgarity my charge had learned since our leaving home, including some choice stable terms picked up from the Manners boys.

"What a bang-up fiddler you are, Stornaway. *I* mean to set up a high perch phaeton one of these days, after I am settled. I would like snow-white prads."

"It might be arranged," he said leadingly. "Mind you, they are shockingly expensive. You would have to be a *very* good girl to earn such a rig."

"He is only teasing," she assured me. "Stornaway knows very well I am floating in grease. I told him last night Papa is very well inlaid, for I think this joke has gone far enough, don't you?"

"Too far."

"I told him I am the greatest heiress in Wiltshire,"

she told me, in no quiet aside, "for I thought *that* would let him know I am not to be trifled with. I am no giggle and squeeze lightshirt, like Phoebe and the others."

"Nothing like them," he said, patting her knee, and winking at me. "You are much better, April." When his hand remained on her knee, I lifted it and set it aside, which was not easy, as I was on the outside of the curricle.

"Well I *am!* I am completely innocent, ain't I, Moira?"

"White as the driven snow," I corroborated, but this excess of protestations was surely confirming him of the contrary.

"I never met one yet who wasn't, under her several layers of soot," he said.

She playfully pushed Lou at him. The animal obliged her by making a sharp claw at his hands. That was how the drive went. I would make every endeavor to return home by some other carriage. Possibly Mr. Leveson might be smiled into offering us a lift.

I set myself to the task of attaching Mr. Leveson as soon as I picked him out amidst the throng already assembled at the beach. Before long, I learned he had come alone in his carriage that would hold four. It was my intention for it to carry three on the return trip.

The seaside was a new experience for Perdita. She had to patrol its border, trotting along at the point where the waves were breaking on the shingle beach, with a squeal and a dash farther inland at each new breaker. Stornaway was not so eager for her company that he added himself to the group of two girls and five gentlemen participating in this game. Neither was Lou-lou. It was I who had the chore of guarding the kitten.

I also had the task of being entertained by a bad-tempered Lord Stornaway, who came and sat at my side to complain about the outing. "I never could understand the lure of picnics," he began, with a bored look about at the group. Some of the youngsters were throwing a ball back and forth, while the more sedate women were already beginning to lay covers and prepare the food.

"Why did you come, then?" I asked, my temper no better than his own.

"Because I am a fool. Food is packed up and carried in baskets out of a civilized house, with chairs and tables and walls, to be served off the ground, while ants and bugs walk all over it. There will be gritty sand in the chicken, the greens will be wilted from the air, the fruit bruised beyond recognition, and if the hostess has any pretention to fashion, there will be melting ices to top it all off. Add the unpleasant and overpowering stench of dead fish and decaying seaweed, and you have a meal to satisfy the greatest gourmet. For that, people leave their homes and drive out to sit in the cold wind."

"With a thoroughly unamusing companion for a savory," I added, pulling a long face, to show my commiseration.

"Just so. Do you refer to the kitten or myself? I see she has stuck you with it."

"I am not so uncivil. I meant *me*. The litany of evils was your own. I enjoy a picnic."

"You are easily amused. I wonder if they have opened any wine yet. Another charming feature of picnics. One is expected to cavort in the wet sand to earn a glass of inferior wine. Folks always bring out their worst wine for a picnic, counting on the atmosphere to conceal its bitterness. I personally take my best champagne, to reward any comers."

"You inflict this form of torture on your own guests as well, do you?"

"Not through choice. Stornaway happens to be within commuting distance of Stonehenge. Folks

134

visiting us from any distance always hint at their eagerness to see a bunch of rocks standing in the middle of a desolate plain. I have been to view Stonehenge nineteen times in the past twelve months."

"What is it like? I have never seen it."

"Dull. Very dull, to *see*. To visit it with antiquarians is another matter, to actually explore it, and try to uncover its secret. I am going to bribe some wine from the servants. Stay here. I shall be right back."

When he returned, he carried a bottle of champagne and two glasses. "I hope you are ashamed of yourself. Champagne, and here you have been forecasting the dregs of the cellar," I chided him.

"It will be very bad champagne," he promised.

"*I* think it's lovely," I said, after tasting it. "Like drinking stars and moonbeams."

"What a romantical notion. I should have got a saucer, to see if we could not get Lou bosky, to be rid of him. Where are you from, Molly?" he asked, when a few sips of wine had helped stabilize his temper.

"Yorkshire, originally."

"You have concealed your origins well. They have such a heavy accent; it must have taken some doing."

"I have traveled about a good deal, but gentlefolks are not so afflicted with the accent as the farmers."

"Yes, you would have heard decent accents in your mistress's household."

"My *mother's* household," I pointed out.

He smiled lazily, but made no reply. "Did you hit the road quite young?"

"Yes, my father was an army man. We were moved about a good deal. My mother and I traveled with him, when she was alive."

The surprised look on his face told me he expected some other answer. His next offensive question cleared the matter up. "How long since you struck out on your own, I mean?"

"When I left home after my mother's death, I went

135

directly to my relatives, the Brodies," I answered, with a haughty stare, refusing to acknowledge his meaning.

"When did you and April join Tuck's outfit?"

"The evening you assaulted Perdita, backstage at Marlborough."

"Assaulted her? My memory is rather of *you* assaulting *me,* with a very heavy reticule."

"I am amazed you can remember any of it. You were thoroughly disguised, and I don't mean just as Mr. Brown, either. Where is your friend, Mr. Stafford?" I asked, to change the subject.

"At his home, in Dorset. He is getting shackled this month."

"Oh really! Who is the girl?"

"You would not know her, Molly. What are your plans, after you leave here?"

"We hope to stay with a relative in another city."

"How wonderfully informative! What city?"

"You would not be interested to know."

"I would not have asked, if I did not want to know. If you have learned anything about me, it must be that I don't mince my words."

"I don't consider that the *foremost* thing I have learned about you, Lord Stornaway, though I grant it to be true."

"You are a difficult lady to hold polite conversation with."

"This is not a polite conversation. It is a combination of insulting questions and an interrogation to try to discover where I mean to take Perdita."

"You fear the relative in an unspecified city might dislike my presence? A Dutch uncle, I take it?"

"Just call him Hans. The champagne was delicious. I mean to go for a walk now."

"Lou and I will join you," he said at once, lifting the kitten from my lap and standing up.

"Don't feel obliged to put yourself to the exertion, Lord Stornaway. I would prefer to be alone."

"Just call me Storn. About Hans—is it already arranged?"

"It is not a matter to concern you."

"But it does, all the same. Is he your patron, or the girl's?"

"We go to a mutual relative. We are cousins, Perdita and I."

"This sounds very bad to me."

"Oh, really! You have an utterly debauched mind. Go away."

"I am one of nature's burrs. I shall stick. But what can you expect at a picnic? Let us walk this way," he suggested, turning in the opposite direction from that taken by the youngsters.

"Perdita went this way," I pointed out, as my main reason was to follow her. I wished only to keep her in view, not catch her up. He followed at my side.

"There is a reason for my questions, you know," he said, looking out to sea.

"Yes, and I have a fair idea what it is."

"It is not April."

"I don't know what chance you may have of recovering your money, but you waste your time following her. I suggest you return to Mother Gaines and beat the other five hundred out of Daugherty, if you actually gave him the sum mentioned."

"I don't lie, Molly."

"Neither do I," I was unwise enough to reply. A blighting dark eye was levelled at me. No words were necessary to make his point. I had promulgated such a variety of stories over the past week that I hardly remembered myself what I had told, or to whom. "Usually," I added, in a justifying way. The blighting eye softened, then soon twinkled into a smile.

"Nobody's perfect," he admitted, with great magnanimity.

The shouts ahead of us grew louder, as a large breaking wave washed over some tardy person's feet. It was inevitable, I suppose, that it should be Perdita who got wet. Part of the group went on, while she ran to a rock to sit down, surrounded by three or four blue-jacketed youths. There was a loud clamor of laughing and teasing, the point of which was that she was about to remove her shoes and stockings, and was ordering her court to turn its collective back to her, to allow her some privacy during the operation. She certainly saw Stornaway and myself approaching, but this did not stop her. She lifted her skirt and began rolling down her stockings. I believe she did it on purpose to regain Stornaway's attention for while I may not have mentioned it, she had first tried to get him to join her on the romp along the water's edge. A white foot, ankle, and about half of her lower leg were flaunted, while she pretended to be unaware of his keen attention.

"Does it also tie its garter in public?" he asked me, in a tone of disapproval. "Even amongst the muslin company, I have not seen such behavior as this."

I went forward to wrench her skirts down, using all my control not to box her ears. Her feet were thoroughly soaked. Water was dripping from her shoes and the hem of her skirt was destroyed with water and sand. There was no way she could make a presentable appearance back at the picnic. I suggested to the backs of the gentlemen around her that they proceed with their walk. Stornaway, with a glance that held some sympathy directed at me, went along with them, still carrying the kitten.

I was in a quandary as to what should be done. In the end, we dried off her skirts as best we could, returned to a spot a little removed from the other picnickers, placing her shoes and stockings in the sun to dry. With some discretion, folks might not have noticed she was barefoot, but discretion was not a large part of her makeup. Before long, she had several sympathizers, every one of them male, and

138

several outraged matrons, interested in her condition.

She sat like a queen bee when luncheon was served, ordering her various drones to bring her a wing of turkey, to butter her bread, to select the finest fruits for her. Mr. Leveson was not about to be drawn into such a low circle as hers, of which I made up a part. He went and sat off with a different group.

I have not made much mention of John Alton in all of this, but he was not forgotten by Perdita. On this, her first foray into Society, she must have the attention of every man. He had taken the precaution of seating himself well away from her, with Millicent, but this did not stop her. It only made it worse. She shouted at the top of her lungs to him at frequent intervals, reminding him of various childish exploits I fancy he would rather have forgotten. He glared, grimaced, pretended not to hear her, and finally shouted for her to stop pestering him. He had rather forget he knew her.

She tossed her tousled hair and said to Bob Manners, sitting at her feet like a puppy, "He is jealous of you."

She fed bits of food to her kitten, then when it had had enough, she pulled its mouth open and tried to force food in. Even the kitten was disgusted with her. It bolted from her arms and ran for cover.

"Get it, Moira! Grab it, before it runs into the sea!" It was actually headed in the opposite direction, scampering up the rocks behind us.

"Get it yourself. She's not your slave," Stornaway said sharply. For a fraction of a moment, I was actually in charity with the man, till I realized she meant to do as he suggested, go running and climbing, in her bare feet, before the whole company.

I pushed her down. Lou Manners saved the day by running to retrieve his namesake.

I cannot speak for the others; I was relieved when some dark clouds began gathering, then blowing in towards us as the wind rose. It made an excellent excuse to curtail the picnic. There had been some races planned, which I had no desire to see my charge participate in.

"Let us get out of here before it pours," Stornaway said, picking up her shoes and stockings, still soaking wet. She extended her hands to him.

"Help me up," she ordered.

"The Lord helps those who help themselves," he replied, and turned his back on her to speak to me. "Another delightful feature of picnics that I forgot to mention earlier. Rain. Inevitably rain before the day is out."

Offended at his rough treatment, Perdita said, "I will not drive in *his* carriage, Moira. I shall return with Lou and Bob."

"Good!" Stornaway said, with real relief.

"I cannot let her go alone."

"Those two strapping fellows can take care of themselves," was his reply. At the last moment, he shoved the wet footgear into Bob Manners's hands, while Lou got stuck with the kitten.

I was not sorry to get away from her for a half hour, to let my pounding head settle down. "I cannot think why you refused *any* offer for that wench," Stornaway said, as he handed me into his curricle.

"Count your blessings. You see what I saved you from, a fate worse than death."

"I want you to know how much I appreciate it. Sure you weren't just saving me for yourself?" he asked with an arch smile.

I was so relieved to see he had taken her in dislike that I did not give him the setdown he deserved. Neither did I give him one jot of encouragement. "No arguments, Stornaway. My head is thumping."

"If you have anything less than a full-blown migraine, it is a miracle. Poor Molly," he said, patting my hand, and showing me a very pretty smile. "I am going to be an exemplary companion all the way back to Bromley Hall. I shan't turn reprehensible again till your headache is gone. Promise."

Good to his word, he conversed in a fairly rational manner till we were back at Grifford's.

Chapter Thirteen

The time before dinner was occupied with the nearly impossible task of getting the tangles and residue of salt out of Perdita's hair, and making her appear less than a hoyden for the evening's entertainment. I also wished to borrow evening slippers for her, and with this end in view, sought out John, hoping he might prevail upon Millicent's patience in the matter. It did not occur to me there might be any irregularity in entering his room. I found him in the sitting room attached, just sitting alone, with a pensive look on his face.

"I did it," he said, in fatal accents.

"Did what?" I asked, thinking he referred in some oblique way to Stornaway, and our predicament.

"Proposed. I am an engaged man, Moira. She said yes."

"Oh! Congratulations, John. She is very nice. You will be happy."

"I suppose you are wondering what I see in her?" he asked, on the defensive.

"Certainly not. You already told me she is very eligible."

"It wasn't the money. Perdie's richer, and I would not take her for all the fish in the sea. Millie is not very pretty, and she's not clever or anything like that. It is just that, somehow, she is *comfortable*. I feel *right* when I am with her. Smarter, braver, better."

"She brings out the best in you."

"That's it. And I like her. She wasn't even mad about Perdie acting the hurly-burly girl at the picnic. I mean to get that chit out of here as soon as possible. Tomorrow morning. I'll drive the two of you back to Mama, and then come back here."

"That's good, excellent. Has Stornaway said anything to you?"

"No, how should he? He never climbs out of your pocket long enough to speak to anyone. He was to meet me in the saloon before lunch, but didn't show up, and I was not so eager to see him that I sent looking for him. It begins to look as though it was *you* he was after all the while, not Perdie. He's disgusted with the brat, like everyone else. You'll talk him around. You might mention the FHC . . ."

"You overestimate my influence with him. He won't leave without his five hundred pounds, but that is not why I am come."

He agreed to approach Millie about the loan of slippers. When I came out of his room a little later, Stornaway was coming down the hall. He looked at me—such a look! "In broad daylight, too!" he said, shaking his head.

"Do you ever get your mind out of the gutter! I only went to borrow some shoes."

"Went to the wrong place. His would be too big," he said, laughing as he went along to the staircase. The wretch thought I had come from an amorous assignation with John Alton!

Perdita expressed the keenest disinterest in the match John had just made. The names of Bob and Lou were often heard as she primped and preened

144

before the mirror. While she was occupied with making faces at herself, I took up my scissors and trimmed three-quarters of the bows from her gown. The evening was not a total success, but it was not quite a disaster. The engagement was the main point of interest. It was announced after dinner, and again after the guests had assembled for dancing, to inform the newcomers of the event. No mention was made of its also being Millicent's birthday, though she did receive some gifts. Perdita's pretty nose was out of joint to have the interest diverted from herself, till she hit on the role of jilted lover. She cast dying glances on John for half an hour or so, speaking of "shattered dreams" and "bleak futures," but when the fiddle and piano started up, she abandoned this melancholy pose for gayer revels.

I trailed dutifully along to the dancing room to keep an eye on her. Stornaway, behaving with suspicious propriety, appeared at my elbow. "This has taken me quite by surprise," he said, with a meaningful look.

"I cannot imagine why! You know Perdita loves dancing, and it is my duty to watch her."

"I refer to Alton's engagement."

"It is not a total surprise. He came here to propose to her, I believe."

"A singularly inappropriate time to have brought a couple of stray women along."

"Thank you, but we do not consider ourselves as *stray women.*"

"Not for long, anyway. Alton will be eager to disencumber himself of any side liaisons, now that he is to be a groom."

"You are familiar with the etiquette in such cases, I imagine. Did your friend Stafford do so?"

"Yes."

"There you are, then. John will certainly resign from the FHC, before you turf him out. It is his only love other than Millicent."

145

"This Dutch uncle you mentioned . . ."

"He is actually a widowed aunt, and I do not mean to give you either her name or location, so pray speak of other things, or leave."

"Now, now, don't be rash, Molly. You are still indebted to me, to the tune of five hundred. I don't forget your obligation so easily. I expect more than a few smiles in return." There was a pause, during which I stared fixedly at the dancers. "Would you like to dance?" he asked.

"No, but if you are eager to show off your superb mastery of the art, I shall be happy to watch."

He crossed his arms and drummed his fingers impatiently on either elbow, while he regarded me thoughtfully. I could not venture into any suggestion of his thoughts. He looked pensive. Finally a frown settled between his brows. "Suit yourself," he said curtly, then walked away. I did not see him again that evening. I believe he went to his room. I was obliged to stick it out to the bitter end, but Perdita's suitors were attentive to her, so that she behaved only poorly, and not outrageously. The Griffords were so happy to have nabbed John that nothing could impair their good humor. Millicent wished to be on terms with her prospective neighbor, Perdita, when she should remove to John's home, and to this end she attempted some friendly overtures. I daresay the knowledge of our departure in the morning did more than anything else to conciliate our hosts.

There was some apprehension in my mind that John's mother would greet us with less enthusiasm in London, now that no match between her son and Perdita was possible. But she was still a neighbor, and could hardly cast us out into the street before we heard from Mrs. Cosgrove. With the departure to look forward to, I got the evening in somehow. There was still the unfinished business of Stornaway and the money, but if we could leave very early, we might give him the slip. He could not break the door down at Alton's place. We had only to deny him entrance till Aunt Maude came to rescue us. He had never mentioned Brighton, in any of his conversations. There was no reason he should think it was our destination. No reason we must ever see him again. It brought a profound sense of peace.

John remained below with the Grifford family for a while after the guests had all left. I prepared for bed, donned one of Mrs. Alton's flannelette nightgowns, and went over our plans for the morrow. The thing to do was to leave very, very early. I would wait till I heard John pass by, and give him the message. I threw my pelisse over my shoulders when I heard his steps approach. I opened the door a crack to confirm it was John. "I must speak to you," I whispered.

He stepped just inside the door. "I have told the Griffords we will be leaving early," he said. "With luck, I can be back here by tomorrow evening. I want to pick up a ring while I am in the city. Tony is leaving tomorrow, too. He knows a spot that will give a good bargain, on tick. He is a capital fellow, really. Pity Perdie had not taken a liking for him."

"Yes, the thing is, John, we want to leave *very early*. Not later than six-thirty, to avoid Stornaway, you know."

"He should be gone by the time I get back tomorrow night, too. This will all blow over. Tempest in a teapot. I hope he don't carry out his threat with the FHC. I'll step along now and speak to him before I leave. He was not half so angry with me today as before. Well, he has learned what manner of creature Perdie is, and will no longer care a fig for all that. Let us settle on six for breakfast, then. We have made our farewells to the Griffords, so that is no problem."

"Six is fine. The earlier, the better."

"You might talk Tony up to Perdie a little, after I

am gone, Moira. He would make such a jolly neighbor for us, and he would have to live with her, for he hasn't a sou to his name."

He left, before I had to reply to this piece of folly. I leaned against the back of the door and sighed in relief. While I rested, there was a light tap on the door. I was sure John had forgotten something. Without a single worry, I opened the door, to be pushed into the room by Stornaway. He came in after me, shut the door quietly behind him, and said, "Parting is such *demmed* sorrow, but you really ought to do it somewhere other than under the new fianceé's roof, you know. Bad *ton*." He held a lighted cigar in his left hand, I noticed.

"What do you want?" I asked, consciously lowering my voice, to prevent any passerby from hearing I had a man in my room. Lord, and they would be bound to smell the smoke, too.

"Same thing as Alton," he answered, with an irrepressible smile. *"You*. We men are all alike, feet of clay."

"Feet! You are clay to the knees. Get out."

"Higher!" he said, the laugh taking on a lecherous tone.

I started to back away. The pelisse slipped from my shoulder. I reached to pull it back. Stornaway's hand came out and whipped it off, tossed it to the bed. I was dreadfully aware of that bed, spread out so conveniently behind us. I turned sideways, so that I might back against the dresser instead.

He lifted his brows to see Mrs. Alton's antiquated flannelette gown on me. At least it was perfectly concealing, more so than my evening gown. "I had not thought Alton would be a *demanding* gentleman, to be sure, but I had thought he would do better than *this* by his women."

"I borrowed this from his mother," I explained, looking for any subject but the one I knew was coming.

"I shan't ask how it came about. A fellow who drags lightskirts along on his betrothal visit would hardly cavil at having them under his ancestral roof. I must confess, though, I find it damned off-putting . . ." he added, with a dissatisfied frown. "Spinsterish!"

"Let us talk in the morning," I suggested, taking a tentative step towards the door, hoping he would follow.

He followed all right, came smack up behind me, and put his two arms around me. "Sure, Molly, we'll *talk* any time you like," he said in a soft, caressing voice, "but *now* . . ." He lowered his head and kissed me on the ear, which has a very peculiar effect on a person. It sent a shiver through me. I jerked away. His hand clamped my wrist in a hard grip.

"Long threatening comes at last, my pet. Time to pay the piper. Now you wouldn't want to set up a scream and scandalize a polite household, would you, Molly old girl? A fine way to repay Alton for his troubles."

"I will scream, if you don't leave," I threatened, but my voice was weak. People know when you are bluffing.

He swung me around to face him, still gripping my wrist. "Time and patience have run out. This tale of procrastinated rape, in the time-honored tradition of Richardson, has reached its climax. I *want* you, Molly."

"But it is Perdita you—bought," I said, stumbling over the awful word.

"I didn't get her, and now I have changed my mind. I want *you*. You sharp-tongued vixens wear better. Am I not an obliging fellow, to let her off the hook? I have concluded you guard her so carefully because she is a virgin. I am not in that line," he said. "You are more in my style." During this bold speech, he let his eyes wander over Mrs. Alton's gown, which cannot have told him much. At the end,

149

he remembered his cigar, took a puff, and blew the smoke out, some of it flying into my face.

"You underbred boor!"

"I had not intended more than having a few words with you at your door, or I would have left my cigar behind. It was seeing Alton slip out that put ideas into my head. I shall get rid of the cigar, if that is what is putting you off."

He did not let go of my wrist as he ground the cigar into the moist earth of a fern on my bedside table. "There is a good deal more about you than the cigar that puts me off, sir."

"Tell me what it is. I am eager to please you. And I think I know how to do it, too. Shall we discuss terms? You have five hundred already. Keep it, as there is no abbess or pimp to pay off. I'll give you a thousand a year during pleasure. I don't care to get into any annuity. I travel light."

"Don't offer me any more insults."

The chin came up, while he looked down his nose at me. "Fifteen hundred, then. That should be an insult to please the most rapacious."

"Get out—now."

"Two thousand per annum. My top offer. Take it or leave it. I cannot believe Alton was half so generous."

"This has nothing to do with generosity."

"Everything has its price. For curiosity's sake, I should like to know your customary one, Molly."

"It has failed to register on your consciousness that I am a woman, not a *thing*."

"I noticed it some time ago. You certainly are a woman, a *magnificent* one, especially when you are angry. I bet they all tell you that," he said, injecting a tone of admiration into his bold voice, while he tried once again to get his arms around me. "Twenty-five hundred," he said, in a coaxing way, his voice growing husky.

"I'll—I'll get the five hundred somehow," I told

him, backing away, but he kept following me. "I'll save it up. It will take a little while. I only make a hundred a year . . ."

"You are not exacting a sufficiently high sum from Alton, or from April's prospective patron, either. Her earnings alone should provide you more than that."

"Miss Brodie does not have *earnings*. She has an income, which Sir Wilfrid handles for her."

"Molly, my dear girl, there is no need for this sham. I like you as you are, flaws and all. I am a wealthy, generous man." There was a reasonable sound in his voice that had not been there earlier. Much good it would do me. He was not willing to listen to *my* reasoning, only his own. "This has been very amusing, a French farce, with lovers darting in and out of doors, but I want to settle the matter tonight."

"Please go. Someone might hear you, and that cigar smoke . . ."

He laughed. "It never ceases to amaze me, how you girls will suddenly take into your heads to discover propriety, at the most implausible moments. Well, this *is* a proper household, and your friend *has* just got himself engaged, so perhaps it will be best to postpone it till tomorrow. But tomorrow, Molly . . ."

Tomorrow I would be gone. "Yes, tomorrow," I said, in a placating way, as I urged him towards the door.

"You agree, then?"

I did not actually say yes, nor even nod my head, but I did not deny it, which he took for agreement. "We'll take April wherever she is going, and I will take you to a place I have, a very nice house," he said. I smiled nervously, wishing he would stop these plans. "We are going to be very happy, Molly. We shall suit admirably. You'll see. Don't judge by the way I have been carrying on with April. I was

151

only vexed at being outwitted by a—by you and Daugherty."

I got him to the door as he spoke, listened to ensure the hall was empty, then opened the door an inch to peek out. "Can't we seal it with a kiss at least tonight?" he asked, but still in a reasonable manner.

"No, I . . ."

"Yes."

I was in his arms, with his head coming down to me. His lips found mine. Believing me to be a professional at this sort of thing, he did not hold anything back. I was subjected to a ruthless, long, passionate embrace that left me weak, breathless, shaken with shock.

"There goes *my* sleep. This is going to be a long night," he said, with a glowing smile, *friendly*. Then he kissed the tip of my nose, and slipped silently out the door.

The most amazing thing about the encounter was how enjoyable was the chore for which certain women were paid staggering sums of money. No, I think there was one item more amazing still—that *I* was considered dashing and desirable enough to qualify. Like Tuck's theatrical performance, one was morally bound to object, to take dire offense in this case, but if one were a legal wife, it would be a different matter. I wondered, as I sat on the edge of my bed looking out at the moon, what Lady Dulcinea was like. I indulged, too, in a little self-pity. Every girl or woman one met, or the ladies at least, were being helped to a husband. Millie's parents threw her a party, Lady Dulcinea's got her Stornaway, Maude would make a good match for Perdita. Who was to act for me? I would obviously not settle for being Stornaway's mistress, but I would look sharp when we got to Brighton. I would find someone, and it would not be an aging widower, either. If Stornaway could admire me as a woman. . . . But it was best to forget Lord Stornaway.

Chapter Fourteen

The sky was just lightening when I awoke, tired, my eyes gritty from lack of sleep. I made a hasty toilette in cold water, noticed Stornaway's cigar butt in the potted fern and threw it out the window, then went next door to rouse Perdita. It took five minutes to get her from her bed. While she complained and dressed, I packed up our few belongings and tidied her room, which she had managed to reduce to an utter shambles. The kitten bounced off a chair in the corner and meowed under my feet. We moved quietly along the hallway to prevent awaking the other sleepers. Already the servants were up. The aroma of coffee greeted us, along with sounds from the breakfast parlor hinting at cups being placed on the table. With a rising sense of urgency, I told Perdita we would have only coffee, to hasten our departure.

"If John is even up yet," she answered, smothering a yawn.

John was not only up but already into a breakfast of gammon and eggs. Millicent sat at his side, looking disgustingly bright and chipper for six o'clock in the morning. I did no more than glance at them. Stornaway was up, too, sitting at the end of the table with an anticipatory smile decorating his face.

I stopped dead in the doorway, my eyes flying to John. The gentlemen disturbed their eating to arise and make us welcome. John had the decency at least to look embarrassed, but beneath the embarrassment was a firm sense of purpose, as he outlined the change of plans.

"It happens Stornaway is going back to London today, girls, and has offered to drop you off at Mama's. It will save me the trip."

With Millicent smiling her approval, it was difficult to enter into the tirade that was building up inside me. Perdita took the offer as another compliment to her own charms. Tired as she was, she cast a coquettish smile on Stornaway as he placed her chair. I said literally not a word, but I had not the least notion of leaving Bromley Hall in any carriage but John's. When I took my seat beside John, he leaned over and said in an undertone, "No need to frown like Jove, Moira. I explained the whole to him. We'll talk before you go."

So eager was I to hear this talk that I had only half a cup of coffee, before making an excuse to return to my room. I cast an imperative stare on John, who joined me in the hallway within a minute.

"You have got to take us, John. You cannot desert us now."

"You misunderstand. We had a long talk last night, the two of us. I convinced him he was wrong about Perdie. He's not going to blackball me with the FHC. Quite a decent chap, really, when you come to know him."

"How did you convince him? He would never listen to *me*."

"You're a woman," was the unhelpful answer. "He listened to *me* right enough. Told him your whole story—about old man Croft, and that trollop Perdie's

154

papa got shackled to, the lot. He is very sorry he acted so awful, wants a chance to apologize, make it up. Now listen to sense, do, Moira. How should I be sending a couple of *actresses* to put up with Mama? Go with him, and I won't have to make that demmed long trip there and back today. Millicent and I were planning to go to visit her Aunt Hazel this afternoon. Rich as a nabob. She might give us a set of sterling silver plate, if we butter her up right."

Even in the midst of my turmoil, I could not but smile at John's new turn for domesticity and acquisition. "You are *sure* he understands? We will be in a fine state if he has gammoned you."

"Lord, Moira, men don't gull each *other*. He knows full well I would be obliged to call him out if he tried anything. Wouldn't care for that, and he on the edge of an engagement himself. Now there is a good point to bear in mind if he *does* try anything off-color. You have only to let drop the name Lady Dulcinea, and he'll fall into line. He wouldn't want that blue sock he's dangling after to hear a hint of his carrying on."

"You think he might try it, then! You have just admitted it."

"I don't. I know full well he won't do nothing havey-cavey, for he told me so. He only wants a chance to make it up to you and Perdie for the way he's pestered the pair of you to death."

As he finished this speech, the others joined us in the hallway.

"All set and ready to go, ladies?" Stornaway asked, in a perfectly polite manner. There was no mischief in his eyes. Really, I thought he *did* look slightly repentant.

"This has worked out very conveniently," Millicent congratulated the group. "Now John and I can begin paying some visits to relatives who have not met him."

"The weather looks good, too," Stornaway pointed out, glancing towards the windows. "We should be in

London by early afternoon. I have an appointment this evening."

After a few more respectable utterances from him, I was convinced he had accepted the truth about us. It would be amusing to hear his apologies and explanations. John and Millicent came out to the front to wave us off.

The apologies were not so amusing as I had hoped. As to the explanation, it was practically nonexistent, but at least he *did* apologize, and behaved with decency. "I am sorry for the difficulty I have caused you both since our meeting," he said as soon as we got rolling. "We all know what caused my misapprehension. The less said of the affair, the better. So, ladies, I cannot believe you plan to remain indefinitely with Mrs. Alton in London. A Mrs. Cosgrove, Alton mentioned as your chaperone. Aunt, is she?"

"She is my aunt, and Moira's cousin," Perdita told him. "We are going to stay with her in Brighton, if she will let us."

"Is there some doubt about it?" he asked, looking startled.

As I firmly declared "no," Perdita said, "Oh, yes," and went on to explain.

I had very little to do but listen during the remainder of the morning. Perdita, her imagination and dramatic instinct activated by a handsome listener, went into a lengthy spiel of her melodramatic background. A tear oozed out as she mentioned her mother's death. Her stepmother was sunk from being a common, jealous female to a positive ogress, who would *force* her to have the libidinous Mr. Croft, and steal her fortune into the bargain if she could.

"Quite like a romantic novel," Stornaway mentioned, properly awed. "Just what is the extent of your fortune?" I measured a calculating stare on him, but his eyes rested on Perdita. We were in his carriage, not the curricle. His tiger drove the latter; he had passed us a few miles before. It was beginning to appear to me the gentleman had a new set of designs on my charge. Whatever Lady Dulcinea might look like, she could not possibly be prettier than Perdita. He had described the lady as dull, which was a charge never levelled at Miss Brodie. In fortune, it was unlikely the noble Dulcinea outranked my cousin. The only other matter up for comparison was behavior; Perdita's assorted tricks had never disgusted any other suitor, once her fortune was known. I supposed Stornaway was not that different from other men in that respect.

"Fifty thousand pounds," she answered sweetly. "And *more* when my Aunt Maude dies. She will leave me her house in Brighton. It is on the Steyne, in the center of town, with a view of the Pavilion. Aunt Agatha will leave me something as well. That is Papa's sister."

"And *you*, Miss Greenwood, have you no fairy godmothers?" he asked, with a little smile, possibly of disbelief, towards Perdita.

"Yes, she has *me!* I shall take care of Moira when she is old," she told him, with a self-righteous face.

"That should set you to trembling!" he cautioned. "You two are cousins, you say. How does it come one is not only an heiress in her own right, but to receive legacies from the aunts as well? It would seem more logical the old girls leave it to *you*, Miss Greenwood."

"They are more closely related to Perdita. Mrs. Cosgrove is only a cousin to me. She is Perdita's aunt. Naturally she will leave her estate to her niece. The other, Agatha, is no kin to me."

"It is not the way estates are managed in my family," he mentioned.

"It is really too bad," Perdita agreed, "and on top of it all, *I* shall make a very good marriage, while Moira will not make any."

He quirked a sympathetic brow at me, then returned his attention to Miss Brodie. If I was not eligible for a mistress, I was of no interest to him. It was as clear as glass.

As the morning wore on and the hour for luncheon approached, Perdita said, "When are we going to stop? I am *starved*. I hope we go to a very fashionable inn. I mean to wear the new bonnet I got yesterday. You will have to get the box for me, Stornaway."

"I planned to stop at my country place," he replied.

"Stornaway is nowhere near here! It is up towards Chippenham," Perdita objected, voicing a fact that had occurred to me as well.

"How the deuce did you know that?"

"You need not think we are flats. We have known ever since Marlborough that you live at Stornaway. Is it a very grand estate? Phoebe made sure it was. She suspected all along you were a lord. Remember, Moira, she said she made a point of calling him 'milord,' and he never batted an eye, but only turned around and answered her."

"The actresses are well organized," he said, looking at her askance.

"It will be best if you forget about the actresses," I told her. "That is a shameful part of your past we shall not draw to anyone's attention in future. As she mentioned, however, Stornaway is not near here, is it?"

"I was not referring to Stornaway. I have a summer place, a weekend retreat I use when I am in London."

"It will not be ready to receive company," I pointed out, disliking to be drawn off our direct route.

"I keep a couple there all year to look after it. I would like to stop and give my servants instructions. Now that I am going to town, they will want to know it, and ready things for me. They can give us a luncheon, at least."

The lack of funds limited our options. When Stornaway was to feed us, it was hardly polite to insist he do so at a public inn. "Very well, but we must make quick work of it," I said.

His place lay just to the west of Tunbridge Wells. It was reached by turning off the main road and traveling down a pretty country lane for about a mile. It was a cottage, no more, but a quaint Queen Anne cottage, with leaded windows and a garden of roses just budding. Behind it, a row of willows streamed their green ropes down, hinting at a body of water. As we approached the house, the glimmer of a smallish river was seen, sparkling in the sun.

"How lovely! It is like a little fairy castle!" Perdita exclaimed. "What do you call it. Stornaway?"

"Birdland," he answered.

The word raised a tumult in my breast. I had heard the name before. It was the singularly appropriate name selected for his love nest, where he had planned to bring Perdita when he mistook her for a ladybird. I expect this nest had seen an assortment of them in its time. But his face was impassive as he rhymed off various larks and robins whose presence contributed to the place's name. I could not like to betray too close an interest in his possessions, nor that I had been listening in on his private conversations.

The house was tended by a respectable-looking couple, a Mr. and Mrs. Steddy, who did all that required doing when his lordship was not in residence. It would be more grandly looked after when it had a regular occupant. They expressed considerable surprise to see him.

"I want to talk to you, Steddy," he said to the man. "Would you be kind enough to take the ladies upstairs to wash?" he added to the woman.

We followed her up a circular staircase, to a long hallway lit by leaded windows at either end. There were six doors, three down either side. "I guess it's the guest room he'd be meaning," she said, opening one door for us. The room was charming. There was

159

old Chinese wallpaper, good furnishings that dated from the same period as the house. We washed rather quickly, and thus returned below before luncheon was prepared.

"Would you like to have a look around the place while Mrs. Steddy prepares some food?" he asked.

I have personally an insatiable curiosity for looking over people's homes. I never reject any offer to take a tour, even when it means laying down money for a hired tour, as is done at Swindon to raise funds for the Historical Society. I was disappointed when Perdita said, "I want to go out and see the river. I'll take Lou with me."

Stornaway had noticed the eagerness on my part. "Let me show *you* around the house, Miss Greenwood. It is rather interesting. Lady Marlborough is said to have designed one of the suites. She was a bosom friend of my ancestor who had the place built. By legend, the desk in that suite was her gift to the hostess for having entertained her."

"I would love to see it," I answered, my interest fanned to a white heat by the story.

We went abovestairs, into a suite of rooms that had a view of the river. There was no Chinese wallpaper here, nor any antique furniture. A stark white textured paper, plastered with gold roses as big as cabbages, hung on the walls. Gold draperies were at the windows, and a gold-canopied four-poster stood in the corner. A gilt cage was erected on top of the canopy; a canary on a perch, a stuffed canary that is, was imprisoned in the cage, from which garlands of flowers were suspended. The Pantheon Bazaar came to mind, in all its gaudy splendor. There was more. A brocade chaise longue stood under the window, with a little table at its side. The floor was covered with a thick white rug, also sprinkled with gold roses. A jarring note was added by a crystal vase holding a bouquet of red silk roses. There was no desk in evidence, from the period of

160

Queen Anne or any other monarch. One felt instinctively the chamber had been done up by an illiterate female, with a bent for finery.

"This is the sitting room in here," he said rather quickly, looking at me in a curious way. Again there was no desk. What there was was a plenitude of mirrors, dressing tables, and mostly clothes-presses. "Lady Marlborough wrote on a dressing table, did she?" I asked, with a suspicious look.

"The Steddys must have moved it," he answered quickly. "But do you like the suite?"

"No, I cannot say that I care for it. It is not to my taste at all."

"You can have it redone any way you like."

"Is it worthwhile to go to so much bother? We should be gone within the hour. Shall we go below now?"

He quietly closed the door, leaned against it and folded his arms. "First, let us have a chat, Molly."

"Moira. Miss Greenwood to you."

"Yes, yes, in public I shall address you any way your delicate sense of propriety decrees, but *entre nous*, my heart, you will always be Molly. I have not the least objection to being styled Mr. Brown, either. In fact, the house is leased under his name."

"A recent transaction, I take it? Your ancestral bosom-bow of Lady Marlborough resided elsewhere? In your imagination, perhaps?"

"Precisely."

As he made no move to unfold his arms or change his posture, I, too, leaned against one of the many clothes-presses and adopted a similar attitude. "You lied to Mr. Alton, and you lied to us. This is what you had in mind all along. Not taking us to London at all."

"I am very eager to unload April, in London or anywhere else you care to suggest. As to *lying*, well, let us say I was undecided. I felt there was one chance in a hundred Alton and you were telling the

161

truth. April's tale removed the one percent. The wicked stepmother and the lecherous suitor already strained credulity, without tossing in untold fortunes, to be showered on her from all sources. That you had been discussing me and my assets with your actress friends in light of a potential patron confirmed it. Phoebe was right. I am rich as Croesus. You have done well to attach me, Molly. I congratulate you."

I looked at his shoulders, and I looked at the door behind them. I did not think it would be easy going past the former, to get out the latter. As I sought about for a sound argument, John's tip was recalled to me.

"Would Lady Dulcinea approve of your taking a mistress so close to the wedding?" I asked, in a reasonable way.

"It has nothing to do with her. I have not even offered for her yet, if it comes to that. She is in no position to issue ultimatums. And neither are you. One dislikes to harp on vulgar money, but there *is* that debt between us . . ."

"I cannot get the money while you hold me here."

A frown gathered on his brow. "What is it you object to? You were Alton's mistress, and God only knows whose before him. What is it about *me* that you dislike?"

"Your taste in decor."

"I only paid for it; I didn't choose the stuff. I have already said you can fix it up any way you please. What else displeases you?"

"Everything," I answered comprehensively.

"Could you be more specific?"

"I could beguile your ear for a fortnight. But let us begin with Lady Dulcinea, the mysterious fiancée. Who is she, by the by?"

"You would like to know that, eh, Molly? What mischief could you not create running to her with

162

stories? You may be sure she is no one you know, or will ever meet. What else?"

"I do not admire your reputation as the greatest rake in all of England."

"Wounded to the quick!" he said, uncrossing one arm to strike his heart. "Since a running visit to France and Italy a while ago, I am generally accorded the title of the greatest rake in all of Europe."

"You actually think that is something to be *proud* of!"

"Whatever you do, do with all your might! I had the lesson of my tutor."

"Rabbits and minks spend their time as you do! Do you have no *serious* concerns?"

"My dear Saint Molly, I am not asking you to spend the rest of your life in bed. I have many other concerns. I only visit Birdland on weekends. Twenty-five hundred per annum is pretty good pay for a weekend job."

"I really cannot understand why you persist in this. I should think pride would cause you to desist, or shame."

"They tempt me to change course, but I have more determination than pride. You are a very clever girl. The unattainable is always what a man wants. You have already managed to put me at a disadvantage, justifying my life, my character, when you are every bit as bad, if not worse. You have more than doubled the price I usually pay, and *still* you quibble. Whatever about my character, I know you like my person well enough. That was perfectly clear last night. Don't trouble to deny it. The attraction was not all on one side. We'll throw in a carriage and pair—you name it. Any number of gowns you want, but I insist on overseeing their selection. I don't want to see you in flannelette nighties." His eyes strayed uneasily to the clothes-presses as he spoke.

"Will I see a sample of your wonderful taste if I open one of these doors? One would take you for a wardrobe master, with such a quantity of them."

"No! Those are just old clothes—costumes for a play . . ."

I opened the door, and stared at an array of perfectly contemporary outfits—evening gowns, riding habits, morning dresses, suits. I lifted one or two at random out for inspection. "What *can* the play have been, I wonder? *Love's Labour Lost,* perhaps, as the woman did not get to keep her wardrobe. I don't care much for your taste, Stornaway. A trifle vulgar and gaudy to suit me. I never cared for swansdown trim. It catches in the nose, you know, and causes sneezing. I am convinced these were selected by a female who enjoys to have a bird in a gilded cage on top of her bed."

He was nibbling on a smile again, in admission of having been caught in yet another lie. "Swansdown is not de rigueur," he mentioned.

We were interrupted by a discreet tap on the door. With a quick look, as if to silence me, he called, "Come in."

It was Steddy at the door. "The wife says lunch is ready," he said, expressing no surprise to find his master behind a closed bedroom door with a single lady.

"We shall be down presently. Is Miss Brodie back yet?"

"She's waiting below. Says she is very hungry." Steddy left, without closing the door. While the man was within hearing distance, I made a quick bolt towards it and got out.

"We shall continue haggling out the details after lunch," Stornaway promised, as he came up behind me.

Halfway down the stairs, Steddy said over his shoulder, "You might be interested to know the Sarnias are in residence, m'lord."

There was a hesitation before Stornaway answered. "The whole family, or only the duke and duchess?"

"They're all there. Have gone to London for the Season, and came down to open up their weekend place, as you did yourself. They have a party with them."

"Have they been to call?"

"They dropped in yesterday. I didn't tell them you was coming, as I didn't know it myself. Should I let them know you are here, or will you go to them yourself?"

"Don't tell them."

Chapter Fifteen

Perdita was already at the table waiting for us. "What took you so long?" she complained, as her eyes surveyed the tasty cold meats and hot raised pies before her.

"Business," Stornaway answered, then sat down to carve a leg of ham. "I used to tremble in my seat when the roasts were put on the table, in case I would be handed the knife," he said, smiling, and appearing to take some enjoyment from the chore now. "That is odd, too, for I had some notion of being a butcher when I grew up. I liked the village butcher; he used to give me all the best bones for my hound."

"What *are* you going to be when you grow up, Stornaway?" Perdita asked. It was a child's question, and not even intended for an insult.

He stared, not at her, but at *me,* as though I had put her up to it. "In the unlikely event that I ever *grow up,* I shall manage my estate, and sit in the House," he told her patiently,

"That sounds very boring," she commiserated.

"So it does. It is why I remain so determinedly youthful."

"It sounds very interesting to *me*," I said, passing my plate along for ham.

The repast was delicious. I ought to have been trembling in my shoes for fear of more bargaining after luncheon, but I was not. I felt in some undefinable way that I had got the upper hand over Stornaway. He was less ruthless, less physical today, more open to argument. His intention was to strike a bargain, not use force, and I had no intention of humoring him by setling on a fee. With Perdita to bear us company, I would not allow myself to be put upon. If he refused to continue on the way to London, we would quite simply run away. We were not so far from the city. Someone would have pity on two ladies in distress, and take us up in his, or preferably her, carriage.

We were quite lively over our meal. "You must own this is preferable to a picnic in the open air," he mentioned.

"Why no, I was looking forward to having champagne and sandwiches in the rose garden," I replied, only to be contrary.

"We can do that too, some weekend," he answered, with a meaningful, secret look.

"Are you having us for a weekend party?" Perdita asked.

"It is my ardent hope," he said. "I look forward to many pleasant weekends at Birdland this season."

"I am very sure you will be here with *someone*, Lord Stornaway, but I cannot promise it will be us," I told him.

"It will be you; I insist." His smile was softly conspiratorial. Looking at him, Perdita took a pique that it was not directed at herself.

"I am not at all sure I will be able to make it," she said loftily.

"So much the better."

A plate of apple tart was brought to the table, along with a pot of coffee. Mrs. Steddy was a good cook, the fare plain, everyday stuff, but well made. I was invited to pour coffee, while our host served the tart. As we raised our forks, there was a loud knock at the front door. Within a minute, Mr. Steddy came bowing into the room.

"The Duchess of Sarnia and Lady Dulcinea are here," he said, in a voice that held some laughter in it. The look too that he shot at Stornaway hinted at a joke, or at least a bad predicament for his lordship. I must own my own emotion was one of sheer glee. How very delighted I was that his fine lady friend was about to catch him out entertaining a pair of unchaperoned females.

Stornaway sat perfectly, rigidly silent for about thirty seconds, trying to look unconcerned. When he opened his lips, he spoke in a languid manner. "Pray ask the ladies to attend me in the front parlor. I shan't be a moment," he said.

Steddy bowed, smirked triumphantly, and left to do as he had been bidden. Stornaway sprang up and into action. "You two go to the kitchen," he said, pulling Perdita away from her apple tart. "Mrs. Steddy will take you up the servants' stairs to hide in a bedroom."

"I will not hide!" my charge declared firmly. "I want to meet a duchess. I have never met one."

"You never will in my house, brat. Molly, take her above, for God's sake, and be quiet."

"Do you suggest under a bed, or in one of the clothes-presses?" I asked helpfully, taking a sip of coffee. "Pity you had not a firescreen. They are used in all the best French farces this Season."

"Very clever, but you must go *now!*" he said, taking the cup from my hand and slapping it on the table. "I cannot have the likes of you seen by the duchess."

"Indeed no! What *would* she think of her prospective son-in-law? Why, she would take the inconceivable idea he is not quite the thing. I wager Lady Dulcinea would not like it, either."

"Go!" he said fiercely.

There was that in his eyes that encouraged us to go, rather quickly. It was not till Mrs. Steddy had sneaked us up the backstairs that the full extent of our shabby treatment was borne in on us. I took Perdita to the Marlborough suite, not that I particularly wished her to see it, but I was curious to give all those gowns a closer perusal myself.

"What did he mean, the likes of us?" Perdita asked, frowning. "John told him who I am."

"He did not believe us."

"Why was he hinting he would ask us back for a houseparty then, if he thinks that?"

"Because he is a rake and a libertine," I answered unhesitatingly, as I lifted an emerald green gown from a hanger, and held it up before me.

"Would Phoebe and Angela not love to get into all these clothes?" Perdita asked, smiling at the gown. "Really it is a lovely outfit, well-made, and the crepe an excellent quality, only of course the style is so immodest."

"Stornaway is generous to his lights o' love," I agreed. I was not envious, but—well, I hardly know what I was, except to know I was angry and offended.

"It is not right for him to marry Dulcinea, when he was only this week wanting to have *me* for his mistress," Perdita said in her righteous way. "He cannot *love* her, do you think?"

"Love her or not, he is eager to keep her good opinion, the wretch. Look, Perdita, there is a boa of feathers to go with the green gown. Something at least to cover one's bosom. White marabou, with some stiffer feathers to give it body."

She picked the feather snake from the hanger and draped it around her neck, tossing the end over her shoulder in a dramatic gesture Phoebe would have envied. She examined herself in the mirror as she did so.

I cannot say which of us hit on our revenge first. I rather think it occurred to us simultaneously. For many a long day now, and more strongly since last night, I had been fomenting at Stornaway's treatment. Perdita's piques did not last long, but she was in a prime one at the moment because he refused to present her to a duchess. She was ripe for mischief. So was I. We had already exchanged a daring, meaningful glance. Each waited for the other to speak first, in order to have someone to blame later.

"It would serve him right!" she said, looking a challenge at me.

"*I* prefer to think of it as a *duty*."

"But of course it is a duty! If he means to offer for Dulcinea, it is only fair she know his true character. And if he does not, then he cannot be so very angry. You take the green, Moira. It suits your eyes. *I* shall have a red, if I can find one."

"You could find any color under the sun in here, but they may not fit. His ladies are larger than you."

"Why do you suppose the women left them behind? Do you think he made them?"

"It would not surprise me in the least."

She found a red creation, too large, but there was a tray of pins on a dresser. My greatest concern was that the callers would have left before we were ready for our grand entrance. The very fact of his entertaining them so politely, and at such length, while we were asked to hide, added to my scorn. We took time to stir our hair, apply rouge, and practice our Tuck accents before sashaying down the stairs, allowing free rein to our giggles and our accents.

There was no hurry. He had ordered tea and biscuits. He sat between a faded hag of a grand duchess and a younger copy of her, with a teacup balanced on his knee and a pious look on his face when we entered. The pious look was the first thing

171

to go, followed quickly by the cup as it fell to the floor.

That one moment was worth every horrible thing that followed. Some demon possessed me. I looked at the outraged matron, who raised a lorgnette to examine us, and I looked at the prissy daughter, who would have been pretty had she not practiced her mother's facial expression. Mostly, I looked at Lord Stornaway, to see a glowering, repressing, furious scowl. His nostrils were dilated with anger, his lips thin. I felt a compelling urge to laugh. He could not do a thing before the duchess.

I flashed a wide smile on them all. "Ain't you going to make us known to your friends, Stornie?" I asked. "Lud, if we're to be stuck in the middle of nowheres alone for the whole entire summer, we want to be on terms with the neighbors. You only plan to come down to see April weekends, you said."

"Damme, you've spilt tea on my good carpet!" Perdita scolded, in a nice, familiar way. Then she looked boldly at the ladies, made an elaborate curtsey, and said, "I'm April Spring, and this here is my Aunt Molly. She ain't really, but Storn says to call her Aunt, for the looks of it. Say good day to the neighbors, Molly."

"Good day to ye," I said, imitating her curtsey, while I allowed my feather boa to fall to the floor. I made an awkward business of retrieving it, blowing dust off its feathers, and finally rearranging it, while April castigated me for the awkwardest malkin ever she saw.

They all sat staring, saying nothing. "Don't be shy, ladies," I encouraged the visitors. "Have you naught but tea and a biscuit to serve the company, Storn? That's poor peck and booze for a genuine lord to be putting on his board. I'll have my wine, if you please. I can have tea any old time. Give the ladies some of my wine. I don't begrudge a glass to callers. Remember now, you promised to keep champagne in

172

the house for us. April is used to the best from her patrons."

Still they were mute, so I marched to the sofa and sat beside the duchess, who moved over several inches to escape me. "I didn't catch the name, dear," I said in a friendly way, "but the servants says you're a real duchess. It's never true!" She blinked, opened her mouth, shut it, and looked to Stornaway for an explanation.

Perdita, not to be outdone, minced to the doorway and bellowed, "Butler, bring us our champagne! The good stuff. We got a duchess here." Then she smiled benignly on the callers.

Stornaway was gasping like a fish out of water, trying desperately to concoct a story to account for us. "A—a friend of mine borrowed my cottage . . . I had no idea . . ." He stopped dead, run out of invention.

Perdita looked to him and giggled. It was for me to refute the story. "Oh if he ain't the one!" I said, nudging the duchess's elbow. "He's been hounding my girl from one end of the country to the other like a fox after a chicken to get her under his protection. We held out till he come down good and heavy. No more working for fiddlers' pay for us, eh, April lovey? Three thousand a year during pleasure, and one upon disagreement. She's a good girl, mind. No business on the side. I stay with her every second, except for the nights Stornaway comes to her. She don't give a straw for none of the fellows but her Storn. She's a very good girl, and *talented!* Sing for the ladies, April."

"What would you like to hear?" she asked with a curtsey. In fact, she curtsied with great grace any time their eyes traveled in her direction.

"That 'Faire, Sweet, Cruel' you was singing with the traveling theater is a nice, proper song, dear. We don't want to scandalize a duchess with nothing too saucy."

173

The duchess recovered her breath and her wits. "I trust you have some good explanation for this spectacle, Stornaway!" she declared, arising up from the sofa, not without difficulty. "One does not expect to encounter actresses—and *worse*—when she visits a polite household."

"There's nothing worse!" I told her. "We was temporarily with a traveling troupe of actors—nothing but lightskirts and trollops, the lot of them. They'd take up with anything that offered, as long as its pockets was jingling. April was too good for them, which is why we was so glad when Stornaway come along. You don't have to tarry to come into *his* parlor. He's the finest gent *I* ever met, with ancestors going back a decade—longer! And generous to a fault. He's setting up a rattler and prads for April—the latest thing."

"For my daily constitewtional," April confirmed, smiling and curtseying, before going to perch on the arm of his chair, with her white fingers stroking his neck.

"Come along, Dulcinea," the duchess said, pinching her lips.

"Dulcinea! Storn, honey, you never mean this is the gel we're going to *marry!*" Perdita squealed. Her next move was inspired. She ran up to Lady Dulcinea, who had said not a single word thus far, and clasped her two gloved hands. "Listen dear," she confided in a chummy manner, "there's no need for hard feelings betwixt and between us. Share and share alike. I don't hold no grudge against you, not in the least. A gent must have kids, as well as pleasure. Between the pair of us, we'll keep this sad rattle in line, see if we don't."

Lady Dulcinea's lips finally parted. "I would not marry this man if my life depended on it," she said, pulling away from Perdita's grip, her face strained with anger. "He is only fit for the likes of *you!*"

I looked to read Stornaway's reaction. He had got

over his anger. The ludicrousness of the affair appealed to him. He was biting back his smile, while a glitter shone in his eyes. "It has been overlooked that I have not offered for you, ma'am," he pointed out. "If you dislike my friends, it is best that we discover it now."

"Dislike them? *Dislike* them? You are beneath contempt, sir, to have subjected me to this."

"No invitation was issued. Had you waited to be asked to call, you would not have been subjected to it, and neither would my friends. My apologies, Molly."

"Never give it a thought, Storn. I've been insulted by better ladies than this pair of . . ."

"We have never been insulted by a *duchess* before, Molly," Perdita pointed out.

"Oh she *is* a good girl. Honest as the day is long, even when it shows to her discredit," I told Stornaway, before rounding on Perdita. "Of course we have been insulted by better, ninnyhammer. Didn't Lady Clive call you a saucy baggage, and she is ten times as fine as a duchess. She owned her own public house, before she nabbed Sir Giles, and she has a sable cape, too," I informed the duchess, with a haughty stare at her black bombazine.

"That is *trew!*" Perdita confirmed, with a little curtsey.

It was the last thing any of us got to say. With an angry huffing and a bustle of stiff bombazine, the duchess was off, her daughter two steps behind her. Dulcinea turned at the doorway and directed one last, accusing stare on Stornaway. Perdita lifted her finger to her nose in a bold gesture of contempt, then laughed loudly. Next she ran to the window to observe their departure.

"Champagne, melord," Steddy announced, arriving with a silver tray.

Chapter Sixteen

"Thank you, Steddy. Just leave it on the table," Stornaway said.

"If there's nothing else you want, I mean to go and catch that rabbit that is eating up the missus's garden."

"That will be all."

Steddy put down the tray and left.

"April, go up and change that ridiculous outfit," he called to the window.

"Ridiculous? How can you say so, Storn? Did you not pick it out and pay for it?" she asked, still assuming her dramatic accent.

"Come along. I must change, too," I told her, as I edged past Stornaway towards the hall.

A hand fell on my wrist, tightened painfully. "You have asked to have champagne opened, Molly. I do not begrudge the expense. I am certain you are well worth the price, but I *do* insist you have a glass of it."

"I'll have some," Perdita offered.

"No, brat, you will not. This is private. Out." He jerked his head towards the hallway.

"I'll go then, but first I must find Lou. I'm afraid he might fall into the river. Cats can't swim, but I don't know if he knows that yet."

Stornaway released my wrist as soon as she was gone. I regarded him closely, wondering that he did not go into a rant at the trick we had played him. His very reasonableness made me fidgety. He poured two glasses of champagne, and handed me one. "Let us drink to the beginning of a beautiful friendship," he suggested, lifting his glass.

"If you refer to the relationship existing between *us*, it is hardly new. But the champagne looks lovely." I accepted my glass and drank.

"I refer to the new relationship. Now that you have managed to give Dulcinea a deep and well-deserved disgust of me, you can no longer refuse to become my mistress. I don't intend to lose you, Mol. Come now, admit you owe me something," he said, in a wheedling way, as he set his glass down on the table.

"On the contrary; I feel the score is settled, at last."

"Think again. Our books are not balanced yet."

"Let the buyer beware. It is not *my* fault if you got no value for your money to Daugherty. As to Dulcinea, I cannot believe she would ever be happy with a man who tries to seduce innocent girls."

"I have never seduced an innocent girl in my life."

"I said *try*, milord. The motive must count for the act."

"You are paddling into treacherous waters there, Molly. There is only the *intention* between us as yet. If it is to be condemned as the deed . . ." He looked at me, with a significant leer.

I put down my glass, ready to flee, but he spoke on in a sane way. "I am not angry about Dulcinea. Not at all. A man must marry someone. Some proper, preferably aristocratic and dowered lady, to carry on the family name and fortunes. It is expected, the

178

thing to do, as folks say, but it need not prevent a man's being happy on the side. Once I had settled on Dulcinea, I knew I would need a *real* flesh and blood woman, to keep my sanity. I have found her."

"Not in me."

He looked a long, searching, not entirely happy look. "Why not?"

"I don't intend to play second fiddle to your wife."

"First fiddle. You will be the love of my life, Molly, my *real* wife, in all but name."

"Let me rephrase that. I don't plan to be part of any musical ensemble you are mentally orchestrating."

"The wife I had in mind was window-dressing, something to satisfy the world. I know social station means little to you. Even when you were playacting, you cast yourself in the role of chaperone, not leading lady. Be my mistress, instead. Forget what I said about a short-term commitment, traveling light. I love you, and I wish I could marry you, but you know it is impossible. We'll be like York and Mrs. Jordan, a *permanent* temporary liaison, semi-respectable, fertile I hope . . ."

"Don't speak of *love* in the same breath with an offer like this!" I said angrily. The word had jumped out at me from his speech, affecting me in a way I could not control.

"Is it *my* fault you are a—what you are? I have no penchant for calling names, but it is ludicrous your taking high moral ground with me in this affair. We are both human, fallible, imperfect—let it rest at that."

There was a dull ache in my heart, and a sense of defeat. I don't know when it happened. I had no respect for Stornaway; he was all I despised. A rake, unfaithful, opportunist and worse, but I loved him. Like John with his Millicent, I felt *right* when I was with him. I regretted that the only offer I would ever have from him was this unacceptable one. Even if my true situation were known, the offer would be no

179

different. "Some proper, preferably aristocratic and dowered lady" was his requirement for a wife. I was none of them, no longer even decently proper. A mistress, raising a brood of illegitimate children, and at the mercy of a self-proclaimed scoundrel was the best I could hope for. I could only repay him in kind, hurt him as he had hurt me. My experience with Daugherty and company showed me the way to do it, and end this conversation once for all.

"If you are sure you love me, Stornaway, but I feel I must tell you everything. The truth is, I am pregnant," I said, casting down my eyes in a semblance of maidenly modesty.

There was utter, total silence from his direction. Curious to see his expression, I looked up at him through my lashes. He was staring, his face cold and hard with anger. For a very long time he stood thus, looking, silent. When he finally spoke, I hardly understood his meaning. "Alton?" he asked. I had to think a moment before realizing he was inquiring for the prospective father. Poor John! This was really too much to saddle him with.

"No! Oh, no!"

"Who?"

"It—I don't know really . . ." I thought of Daugherty and O'Reilly, but disliked to put myself in such a low category.

"The possibilities are infinite, are they? Any of the Browns or Joneses who were entertained in the Green Rooms? It seems you have given yourself to everyone but me!"

I became frightened at the temper that was mounting in him. There was an angry flush rising from his collar. I backed away a step. "I am leaving now," I said.

"The hell you are!" He grabbed me, in such a fit of passion that I feared he meant to strike or strangle me. I tried to push him off, which only incensed him the more. I was pulled to the sofa, the two of us wrestling like a pair of professional men. I became seriously alarmed, fearful for my very life. I knew Perdita and Steddy were outside, but hoped to bring Mrs. Steddy to my defense. I opened my mouth and hollered as loud as I could.

"Help! Help!" I screeched. His hand came over my mouth, closing it violently. I wrenched my head aside and screamed again.

This is how she found us, Perdita. She was on her way back into the house, with Lou in her arms. She looked a fright, in that awful red gown. She looked, made some muffled sound, dropped her kitten and left, ran back outside. I called after her, not able to believe she would desert me, in such dire straits as this. Stornaway had seen her, too. The sight of another person had the marvelous effect of bringing him to his senses. He loosened his grip, but was still dangerously angry. It was less than a minute before Perdita was back. She advanced, very calmly, with her hands behind her back, and a grim, determined look on her face. It occurred to me she had gone for a weapon. I hoped it was a good stout stick or a rock.

It all happened so fast, there was no stopping her. She whipped her hand out, holding a pistol. She raised it, her hand trembling, causing the gun to wobble. "Don't!" I shouted, just as Stornaway leapt up to try to get it from her. He was directly in her line of fire. There was a sharp clap that sounded like thunder at close hand; there was one little leap of flame, then Stornaway lay very still on the floor. He had not uttered a sound as he fell.

"My God, you've killed him!" I could not move from the sofa. I sat, frozen like a statue.

She dropped the gun, nearly hitting him. "It was self-defense!" she said. Through the fog enveloping me came the realization that *I* was to be the murderess. At the moment, it did not seem to matter much. I willed myself to stand up, to go to him.

I bent over his immobile form, where he lay,

crooked, on the floor. There was a hole in his jacket, with blood oozing from it. I found I could not touch him. "Get Steddy. Call the doctor," I said, in a hollow, stranger's voice.

It was Perdita who kept her head, who tried gingerly to open his jacket, to see what damage she had done. A very cursory examination showed her the wound was beyond her powers of helping, and still I could not touch him, not in any helpful way. I took his hand, as I crouched there on the floor beside him. The Steddys came, man and wife. The husband was sent off for a doctor, and still I could not seem to move. Mrs. Steddy ran to assemble hot water, clean bandages, basilicum powder, to ready a bed for him abovestairs.

"Sit down. Have a glass of that wine, miss," Mrs. Steddy suggested, drawing me to the sofa. "Fainting away won't help."

"He is not dead, Moira," Perdita told me. She was sobered to a state of fear and concern. "I didn't kill him. Why was he fighting with you?"

I patted her hand, speechless, then got up and went back to Stornaway. I stayed with him till the doctor came. The two men carried him upstairs. There was a deal of rushing about the house, during which Perdita was of very little help, and I of none at all. I had time for every sort of remorse. I had been criminally irresponsible to have set out on this course from the beginning. I should have taken Perdita back home when Aunt Agatha did not come to Chippenham. Nothing but evil had come of my action. I had submitted her, an innocent child, to the company of infamous people. I had ruined her, and my own, reputations. I had killed Stornaway.

"If there is a trial, Perdita, I did it. *I* shot him."

"No, I did it. Moira, is there such a thing as governess-defense? I mean, it was not really self-defense, but I was defending you. He looked as
182

though he meant to kill you, or was trying to rape you. Which was it?"

"I don't know, my dear. Neither one has been tried on me before."

"He really *is* wicked, isn't he? You were right to warn me. I never thought him to be *this* bad. It has taught me a lesson I shan't forget, ever. No matter how nice and obliging men *seem,* if they are called rakes in the world, I shall know how they can turn."

"Yes, he is wicked. And I am worse."

"I am the worst of the lot," she said, but not with her customary pride at being the most. She was very downhearted.

Chapter Seventeen

It was a long, long afternoon with nothing to do but wait. "Should we not send for his family?" I asked Mrs. Steddy. "In case . . ."

"It's not so serious as all that, miss. He'll pull through. Her ladyship don't know about this place, and he'd rather keep it that way."

"Did the doctor say he would live?"

"Oh, aye, he did. He don't want him moved an inch though. Steddy is in the dismals he ever let the girl have his gun. He thought she meant to take a shot at the rabbit, you see. That's how he come to do it."

The doctor descended, his face sober but not totally despondent. He carried his black bag. He approached Mrs. Steddy to give her instructions. Perdita and I went along, to learn if there was anything we could do. "He'll need plenty of care. Lost a good bit of blood, but he's young and healthy. I've written up instructions for you, Mrs. Steddy."

"I want to help," I said. The news that he would recover was better than a tonic. It was a chance to make up for some of my crimes.

"You would be the young lady he spoke of. His

lordship wants you and the other girl to leave immediately. He is very insistent upon it," the doctor said.

"We cannot leave. He needs every help."

"The Steddys can help him. I shall come by a couple of times a day at first. It was his last word, before the sleeping draught took effect, that the young ladies were to be taken to London, today. He has given Steddy instructions exactly how it is to be done."

"You mean he is asleep! We won't be able to speak to him before we go?"

"He won't awaken for a few hours. It will only upset him if you are still here. He does not want to see you, ma'am. If you are worried about his lordship pressing charges, you need not. He explained that it was an accident," the doctor told me, but with a knowing look, and a rude one, telling me tacitly we were not worth protecting.

After this speech, I went to sit on the sofa with Perdita till Steddy came down to outline the plans for our remove to London. "The wife will go with you in his carriage, for the looks of it. She is to stay overnight at his London house, and come back next day. He asked me to tell you he is sorry, Miss Greenwood, to beg your pardon."

"Sorry?"

"About the misunderstanding. He said you would know what he meant, and he don't believe a word about Browns or Joneses, or Alton—that it was all a hum. It don't make much sense, does it? On t'other hand, he was not delirious."

"What can it mean?" Perdita asked, her brow pleating in confusion. "I think it is a trick, Moira. I don't trust him." The pendulum had swung from no caution to a foolish excess of it.

"We must wait till he awakens and find out," I suggested, with a wary look to Steddy. He nodded his head in satisfaction.

"He won't like it—much!" He cocked his head on the side and winked.

I do not know what Steddy made of it, but to me there was no mystery. Stornaway did not believe my story about being pregnant. His concern for our getting to London before nightfall suggested he had even come to believe the rest of our claims, that we were ladies in distress, creatures to be protected, and not a pair of the muslin company. He knew their way of dealing very well. They did not take steps that were likely to throw them in the path of the law. Who ever heard of a lightskirt shooting a lord, in defense of her own or her sisters' tarnished virtue? Only a lady, or at least a bona fide gentlewoman, would behave so properly!

"Let us leave while we can," Perdita suggested, rather strongly. "He said he would not press charges. Let us go to Alton's, Moira. We can write from there and see how he goes on."

"Maybe *you* should go to London."

"I will not leave you *alone* with him, after what he was trying to do!"

"Stay, then. The fat is already in the fire. Things cannot be much worse for us."

"No, but they could be better, if we went to London," she answered.

After all my remorse at having led Perdita astray, I was tempted to take, or send, her to London. But I had wronged more people than just her. Stornaway too had been misled, and nearly killed into the bargain. It would really not do to have Perdita singing this ballad through the city, as she might well do, once she got away. She could come to no harm here now, with Stornaway flat on his back, and myself to watch her. At the back of it all, of course, was the purely selfish desire to hear what he had to say now that he knew I was not Molly, but a woman who was half respectable at least.

At five-thirty Mrs. Steddy served us a light snack.

At six Steddy took a bowl of soup up to Stornaway. I meant to go up when the bowl was brought down. I depended on Steddy to let him know we had not left, to prepare him for the sight of us, after having been ordered away.

My hope was that Perdita would remain below. To my surprise, she did not offer to join me. She had been jolted into such a fit of caution she did not even want to *see* a rake. "If you need me, just shout, Moira. I shall be within hearing, right here in the parlor."

"I can handle him, now that he is half dead."

"He might have a gun," she mentioned, perfectly serious.

"I don't think so. Steddy took it away."

My fear, when I saw him, was not for my safety, but his own. He looked deathly pale, as he lay on the pillow with his eyes closed. I advanced quietly towards him. One eye opened, to regard me diffidently. He lifted his hand, held it out towards me. I put mine in it. For a moment we remained silent, looking self-consciously at each other, not knowing what to say.

"Thank you for staying. You shouldn't have."

"I know. I wanted to make sure you are still alive."

"Only the good die young. I am not much good, am I, Molly?"

"You are going to be all right."

"You know what I mean."

"Don't try to talk. Rest. Save your strength."

For about a minute he followed my instructions, closing his eyes. I was becoming uncomfortable, leaning over the bed, and looked around for a chair. His eyes opened and gazed at me. "Is there something worth saving it for?"

"Of course there is. You have got several years of hellraking to do yet."

"With you? Otherwise I shall just cock up my toes and go now."

"I am going to get a chair. I have a crick in my back."

"Bring it close. Very close. I want to hold your hand."

I pulled it up till it was touching the side of the bed. He smiled, and reached for my hand again. "You are not the sort to kick a fellow when he is down, so I am going to indulge in a little self-booting, all right?"

"Kick away."

"If you get too disgusted, just call April to pull the trigger again."

"She is waiting below with the gun cocked."

"Good for her. You were right about me. I am every worthless, despicable thing you said. Born to privilege and wealth, and never did a worthwhile thing in my life. I had too much, too soon, too easily always. I took what I wanted, and when I was through, tossed it aside without a thought or care. I never *did* grow up, which is probably why Perdita's penetrating question at noon made me so violently angry. It sounds a hedonistic enough life, but you would be surprised how little happiness it has brought me. Like being at a fair for years. I had begun to realize it, had determined to settle down, get married, do all the proper and expected things."

"Don't fatigue youself. You are talking too much."

"No, please, hear me out. I want to get it off my chest. The Catholics know what they are about, confessing their sins and wiping the slate clean. You are to give me absolution when I have finished. You will not be so heartless as to beat me in my weakened condition. It is now or never. There was no one I wanted to marry, so I chose the belle of the Season, Dulcinea. Top of the hill, daughter of a duke, rich, a *good* girl, you know, not my sort at all. Perhaps that is why my decision fell like a noose around my neck.

189

Stafford and myself discussed it many times. He reached the watershed at the same time as me, both headed for the altar. Then I met Perdita, and you, on our last wild spree. That is all it was to be, just one last fling. I did not want to get tied up in anything lasting. It was extremely disobliging of you to come into my life so late, Miss Greenwood, and in the disguise of a scarlet woman, to fool me."

"The thing is, while you were having your last fling, we were having our first. It was a wretched muddle, from first to last."

"But think if we had not met at all! That must be our consolation. You were the first thing—lady!—I ever came across that I could not have. It first intrigued, then enraged me, and finally convinced me that I *would* have you, whether you wanted me or not. Well, I was conceited enough to think you *did* want me, actually, but were only being a little distant to bring me to heel. It is a good thing I am flat on my back, or you'd knock me over. I see it in your eyes. My behavior has been unforgivable," he said, then looked at me expectantly.

"There were reasons . . ." I said, in an exculpatory way.

"Really I am waiting for more than absolution. You are supposed to tackle that metaphysical impossibility now, forgive the unforgivable."

"Bear with me a moment. The impossible takes longer than a second."

"I may take a turn for the worse at any moment. I see the Grim Reaper in the corner there, hiding behind the curtain."

"That is a shadow, Stornaway."

"Even the shadow of death is enough to set a fellow trembling and making all manner of good resolution. But I mean to keep them!"

"Very well then, I shall forgive you, if you forgive me."

"You mean her, the brat. I not only forgive her, I
190

laud her good sense and resolution. Also her aim, but I think that was an accident."

"It was. She never held a gun in her hands before. She did not mean to hurt you."

"No, she meant to kill me painlessly. How did you come up with that *wicked* idea to tell me you were *enceinte?* I had already turned you into a virginal lightskirt, in my mind. One tumble from the pedestal, perhaps two at the most. Then to hear you say you *didn't know* who the father could be . . ."

"Daugherty taught me the trick. He let on to me he had gotten rid of you at Kingsclere by that ruse, claiming Perdita was in such a state. Did you really give the old faker a thousand pounds?"

"Yes, you know what happens to a fool and his money. But I got nearly half of it back."

"Maybe I could go to Mother Gaines and . . ."

"No! Stay away from him! I will be happy to sponsor the arts a little."

I could see he was upset by my visit, becoming more excited than was good for him. After a short while, I arose to make my leave.

"You must go first thing tomorrow morning," he said. "No one need know you were here the night. We shall put about the impression you went directly from Grifford's to Alton's. I shall call on you there, as soon as I am able."

"We won't be there long."

"Let me know where you go, then—Brighton, or whatever. We shall discuss it tomorrow before you leave."

"All right. Good night." I leaned over to pat his hand, as anyone will do to an invalid.

He grabbed my fingers, squeezed them. "I wonder if I have a fever. Would you mind feeling my brow?"

It felt warm to my touch. "A slight alteration," I told him, concerned, though not alarmed.

"My heart is palpitating too. Feel my heart." He moved my hand to his heart and held it there, at

191

which point I realized he was not so much ill as bent on flirtation, even when he was flat on his back in a sickbed.

I turned a knowing, discouraging eye on him, while searching my mind for a setdown to humor an invalid. My fingers felt the strong, rapid beating of his heart, with not a sign of a palpitation. His good arm reached out, encircling my waist. "Now for the lips," he continued softly, as he crushed me against him for a passionate embrace that raised my own temperature higher than his, and set my heart to wild palpitating.

"You are not feverish; you are deranged," I said severely, pulling myself up, with some disappointment that he was not well enough to overpower me.

"No, I have come to my senses. Sleep well, Molly."

"I shall, if the canary on top of Lady Marlborough's bed does not keep me awake."

"They didn't put you in *that* room!"

"Why, I understood it was the one especially selected for me!"

A light laugh followed me out the door. "No, for *us!*"

Chapter Eighteen

I was in no hurry to court sleep. I had much to consider, as I lay in the fancy canopied bed, beside Perdita. Her restlessness did not help, either. Despite Stornaway's willingness to call the shot an accident, she was envisioning herself on trial. "You must take your place in the dock and defend my good name, Moira," she said, in her heroine's voice, relishing every ridiculous moment.

"You would enjoy the notoriety of being a murderess, but there will be no trial. An accident occurred."

"I did it on purpose!"

"It was an accident that you hit the target."

"I think it ought to be reported."

"If you say *one word,* Perdita, your father will come straight to London and take you home to marry Mr. Croft."

"He would not have me, after this," she said, quite happily.

Eventually she slept, which left me free to build all manner of conjecture on my recent conversation with Stornaway. Being no heroine myself, I was not obliged to misunderstand his intentions. I did not fear for a moment that he would change his mind, call the police, or say a word in Society about our scrape. Neither did I believe he would continue wooing me unless he intended to do the right thing. He was not perhaps so worthy a gentleman as one could wish, but he was not an outright scoundrel. I was besotted enough to believe his professions regarding reformation.

My concerns really centered on other people than Stornaway. A man in his position would be surrounded by a large family, who had very likely higher ambitions for him than marriage to a governess. His near-engagement to Lady Dulcinea hinted at it. He had not courted a lady whom he obviously did not like above half without some prodding from home. He had mentioned a mother, long ago at Marlborough. A large party she had been throwing, so she was a social-conscious lady. A countess might well take exception to a woman who had been in close contact with actresses. Then, too, there was the ill-advised run-in with the Duchess of Sarnia and her daughter, who were a part of Stornaway's social circle. What would *they* have to say of the earl's marrying such a creature as myself? Plenty, when their own daughter was jilted into the bargain.

If wise counsel prevailed with my beau, he would gracefully back out of my life, and I would not throw a rub in his way. He had not actually asked me to marry him. I relied heavily on his lack of wisdom. If he was inclined to the folly of offering, I would not say no. On that determination, I slept very soundly.

When we went below in the morning, our first question was for Stornaway's condition. "He slept like a top," Steddy assured us. "He wants a shave before you ladies go up to say good morning."

This sounded hopeful, that he wished to show us his most handsome face. Before the shave was commenced, the doctor arrived with his black bag. He lowered his brows and scowled, to see us still in the house, after having been invited to leave.

"This will be a fine welcome for Lady Stornaway," he said stiffly.

"She is not coming. She does not even know about Birdland," Perdita told him.

"I felt obliged to inform her," the doctor answered. "The Duchess of Sarnia suggested it."

I did not bother to inquire his business at Sarnia's place. He had run to them to begin spreading the scandal, if I read the man's character aright.

"Is his mother in London, or at Stornaway?" I asked, to gauge how long it would take her to arrive.

"She was in London. She should be here shortly. She could not like to set out last night in the dark, but promised she would come first thing in the morning."

I quickly considered what was best to be done. That dame was bound to dislike us. To find us in her son's house, after remaining overnight unchaperoned was not likely to appease her in the least. Our best course was to be gone before she arrived.

The doctor bowed briefly, then went upstairs. I called Steddy at once. "We are leaving for London immediately," I told him, and went on to explain my reason.

"Stornaway knows our destination. Tell him we have gone, and why. Don't bother to accompany us, Steddy. Stay with him; he may need you. We shall take Stornaway's carriage and groom, and send them back as soon as possible."

"It might be for the best," Steddy agreed, after a little considering. "His lordship ain't in high enough gig to take any extra scoldings today. I'll tell him what happened."

Our packing did not take longer than ten minutes. When we came down, the carriage was just being driven forth from the stable. We clambered in, and the horses sprang into motion.

The day could not have been finer. The new leaves were forming green arches overhead, and in the distance, the river sparkled gold and orange. I had been looking forward to the day at Birdland, but had soon switched my thoughts to excuses that would pass muster with a thoroughly disgruntled Mrs. Alton, and disgruntled she would be at John's engagement to anyone other than Perdita. Miss Grifford was a good catch, but a better one from one's own neighborhood had more appeal for her. Who would know, at Swindon, that John had nabbed a prize heiress? What would the name Grifford mean to them? Nothing, whereas the Brodies had the charm of social superiority at home.

We arrived about fifteen minutes after John's letter telling his mother of his engagement. She was in such a temper she scarcely made us welcome, but when we came downstairs from refreshing our toilettes, she had simmered down to vexed acceptance, and wished to learn second-hand what she could of her prospective daughter-in-law and her family.

"Is she a pretty gel?" she asked eagerly.

Pretty was not, alas, the word that occurred to one in describing Millicent. "She is not ugly," Perdita admitted. "Plain I would say, would not you, Moira?"

"Better than plain. Very nice eyes," I said.

"Do they live in a good style?"

"A handsome house. Everything of the first stare," I said quickly. "Sociable—they had a large party when we were there."

"Who attended it? Anyone I would know?"

The names given were not familiar to her. It was not really friends or acquaintances she hoped to hear of, as it turned out, but titles and celebrities, of which there were none save Stornaway, whose name we deemed it wise to withhold.

After half an hour of lamenting, she decided to like the news, and put on her bonnet to impart it to her cronies. We were invited, but not urged, to join her. I explained we should stay home in case Mrs. Cosgrove came while we were out. I was becoming edgy at not hearing from her. Surely there had been time for one of my letters to have reached her, and for her to have come after us. For the remainder of the day we sat waiting, Perdita and I, jumping a foot from our chairs every time the knocker sounded. It sounded steadily all afternoon, as word of John's engagement was circulated and friends called to see whether they were to condole or congratulate the mother. By three o'clock Millicent had become "a very pretty, well-behaved girl." By three-thirty she was "a considerable heiress, of course," and by four the tale was being promulgated that Mrs. Alton had hoped for just this alliance for some time. Perdita and I were introduced as friends from Swindon, just waiting for our aunt to call for us, and take us off to Brighton.

There was even a little impatience creeping into the last speech, for Mrs. Alton expressed the wish of going to Bromley Hall, where John had asked her to go and meet the family. To her last caller, she said quite frankly she would leave early in the morning, as soon as the girls left. I did not like to consider what would become of the girls if it were impossible for them to leave. It *did* seem an imposition to remain on in an empty house, yet I confess I had not the gall to ask her to take us to Brighton. One can expect only so much good will from neighbors.

It was with an inexpressible wave of relief that the accents of Maude Cosgrove were heard in the hallway while we sat awaiting the dinner bell. I think those accents were a mixed blessing to Mrs. Alton, who would have preferred to hear them before her table was set, but she was relieved to be decently rid of us.

Aunt Maude was wise enough to know we were in some unmentionable scrape, and discreet enough to delay her close questions till we had said good night to our hostess, and got our three heads together abovestairs. Mrs. Alton invited Aunt Maude to remain overnight, it being understood we were all to rise early and go on our separate ways.

"Pray tell me *exactly* what is going on, Moira," Mrs. Cosgrove said, plopping on the edge of her great bed with a sigh of relief. "I have not slept in the same bed two nights in a row for a fortnight, with galloping about the countryside looking for the pair of you. I dashed to Swindon the day I received your letter about that *vile* Croft person, to give Sir Wilfrid a piece of my mind. I had heard my sister mention him as a debauché twenty years ago. He can *not* have been serious to think of marrying Perdita off to such a creature."

"Oh but he was, and it was all my stepmother's doings," Perdita answered for me.

Aunt Maude is thin, fashionable, dark-haired and fair-skinned. I should think she was beautiful a few decades ago. She is still not unattractive. "That vulgar woman!" she said scornfully. "It is enough to make a body doubt Sir Wilfrid's sanity, to see him kowtow to her. But why did he send you to Agatha, instead of to me? He knows I have been wanting to have you for an age. You must be presented properly, in London, Perdita."

"I would *love* it of all things, Auntie!" my charge coo'd, her eyes lighting up magnificently at the suggestion.

"It was pure spite, his sending us to Agatha," I answered. "He was so furious at my talking him out of Croft that he sent us to Agatha to show us a lesson."

"I would not put it a peg past him, but still I do not know how it comes you are in London, instead of at Bath, or back at home. We were frantic to learn you were not with Agatha. Sir Wilfrid sent me packing merrily off to Bath, and Agatha—who is making a great piece of work about a set of sniffles—assured me you were put off by a letter from her at Chippenham. Back to Swindon I go, to be told you never returned. Now, where *were* you?"

"We went to you, Auntie," Perdita said, in her ingratiating way. "We came on to London to Alton's, and John took us to you, but you were not at home, so we stopped off a few days with his new fiancée, then came back here."

"I sent letters all over, so you would know where to find us," I added, hoping she would be satisfied with this sketchy tale.

"I am happy to hear you behaved so sensibly," Maude said, more or less satisfied. Neither Perdita nor I could prevent a quick, smiling exchange of glances at this speech. "But then one can always rely on *your* sound judgment, Moira. You had no trouble along the way?"

"None of any account. Not worth mentioning," I said, my voice high with the strain.

"I see the two of you laughing up your sleeves. Some hedgebird or other was dangling after this minx," she said, with a sly look at her niece. "I am sure you took good care of her," she added to me.

"I trust she is not quite ruined."

As I thought of the possible difficulties Maude might encounter in presenting Perdita to Society next year, I braced myself to give some indication of trouble. The Lady Dulcinea or her mama, for example, might trace a resemblance to April Spring in her.

"There was one unfortunate incident," I admitted.

"I knew it! I saw the two of you biting back your smiles. Let us hear it."

"There was a gentleman at Grifford's houseparty who drove us to London, by an indirect route. We stopped at his summer home for luncheon and there was a—an accident. He got shot, in the shoulder."

"Good gracious! I hope he was not killed. How did it happen?"

I jumped in, before Perdita could take center stage. "His handyman was shooting rabbits, and somehow or other Stornaway got hit by mistake."

"*Stornaway!* You never mean you had the temerity to crawl into a carriage with *that* rattle! You were fortunate it was not yourselves who were shot. But you could not know anything of the man's character, of course, living way off at Swindon. He is not the sort of gentleman you ought to have anything to do with, girls. I hear all manner of tale about his mama, who is a bosom-bow of the Prince Regent, you must know. She is often at the Pavilion, in Brighton. Stornaway and his set are wild."

After this outbreak, I gave no more details concerning our relationship with him. "He was good enough to loan us his carriage to come on here without him in any case," I said, trying not to show my indignation.

"You must not speak too hard against Stornaway, Auntie," Perdita said, with a mischievous smile. "Moira has a tendre for him, I believe. Unfortunately, it was *me* he fancied, but I do not care for him."

"Wise girl! I had as lief see you shackled to Croft. We will keep you away from the likes of Stornaway when we present you. However, there will be no difficulty in that. He is on the verge of marrying Sarnia's daughter, if one can believe gossip."

"The Sarnias have a better opinion of him than you do then, have they?" I asked, hearing and disliking the tone of pique in my voice.

"Not in the least. It is a marriage of convenience. He is rich and noble—that is all that matters in that tribe. His own family the same. They are all cut from the same bolt, the nobility."

Her words sat heavily on my heart. "I hope Stornaway behaved himself?" she asked, looking pretty sharp at my expression.

"Moira kept him in line," Perdita said, with uncommon reticence. "I am happy to have met him, as it gave me some knowledge firsthand of how rakes act. I had been cautioned, of course, but *now* I shall recognize one when I meet him, and avoid him."

"He *did* behave badly, then! What did he do?"

"Nothing really. He was always flirting, and complimenting me," Perdita said. "Once he tried to kiss me, but Moira wouldn't let him."

"It is only to be expected. Well, girls, it is over now. We shall leave for Brighton tomorrow. Sir Wilfrid knows you are to stay with me, both of you. I could not do without you too, Moira. After we have popped this young Incognita off, you and I shall settle down happily. There is no saying we won't find a parti for you at Brighton as well. The older bachelors and widowers assemble there, you know. I do not refer to Prinney's set. There are decent persons going to Brighton as well, now that it has become the fashion. You are looking well, Moira," she added, examining me more closely. "*Very* well. A sort of a glow—the fresh air of spring must account for it. Yes, certainly we shall find a decent man for you."

The prospect of a decent man seemed remarkably tame and unsatisfactory to me. I wondered when I might expect to hear from Stornaway. No, really, I wondered *if* I would hear from him at all. Under his mother's persuasions, he might be talked out of even sending a note, to render excuses for not seeing us again.

Chapter Nineteen

Brighton was jolly in the spring. We did not actually get invited to the Prince's Pavilion, nor would we have been taken if we had. Mrs. Cosgrove held the Prince and his set in great contempt, but we drove past it several times, to admire its domes and gilt, and gardens. We also went shopping, went to Donaldson's library, went for walks and drives along the coast. We were introduced to Maude's set, which was enlarged now to include the sons, brothers and nephews of her own cronies. Perdita was soon the leading belle of the city. Her coterie grew quickly to a throng, then a crowd, and finally a squeeze to fill the saloon. Sir Wilfrid sent money from home, Maude sent to Chippenham for our trunks and to pay the bill at the inn, our debt to the Altons was discharged. All loose ends were tied up except for my friend at Birdland. Plans were always afoot to advance Perdita in the world.

"I *do* believe I shall present her in London in the fall, Moira," Maude revealed one afternoon. "She is better behaved than I hoped. She has no love for rakes and rattles, as a young girl will often do. You did a good job of rearing her."

"Thank you. I did my best for her."

"You are sad at the prospect of losing her. You have scarcely smiled since you came. You are losing that healthy glow you had in London. Cheer up, my dear. Your useful days are far from over. You and I shall deal famously after she is married."

With such an incomparable as Perdita under the roof, any further mention of finding a bachelor or widower for myself had been forgotten. Even the bachelors and widowers preferred her less mature charms. But the real reason for my lack of smiles was, of course, that no word was heard from Stornaway. Ten days had passed since leaving Birdland, more than enough time for him to have written. Even long enough for him to be back on his feet, to have come in person. That gesture suited his flamboyant and romantical nature. In my mind, his hellraking had been smoothed over to flamboyance and romanticism, you see.

I mentally set fourteen days as the longest duration I would go on waiting and hoping. It was on the evening of the tenth day that Mrs. Cosgrove mentioned, very casually, that "that Stornaway fellow" had been to call while we were out, but she had not encouraged him to return.

My heart flipped over in my breast. "What did he say?" I asked.

"He inquired for her—you, both of you. I told him you were both fine, and that I would convey his compliments. He will not be back. He is not slow to grasp a hint; I'll grant him that. He puts up at the Pavilion, you know, with his mama. The countess is a shabby, fast lady. They say she and the Prince performed a duet at the Pavilion last night. Stornaway left off cards for us to attend a party there this evening, but I threw them out."

The Prince and the Pavilion were much discussed by Maude's set of friends. They disparaged everything about it, but in that eager way of the outsider who would, in fact, give an eyetooth to get in. I was astonished to hear she had thrown the tickets into the dustbin, till I saw that they had gone instead into the corner of the framed mirror just inside the front door, for her callers to stare at. "Oh, could we not go?" I asked.

Her dark eyes slid hungrily to the corner of the mirror. "It would do well enough for you and me, but I cannot like to take Perdita there. Truth to tell, I should like to *see* inside it myself. Gretta Norton went once, and never stops boasting of it. I have never been in. One hears marvelous, incredible tales of its splendors, and certainly the exterior is a wonder. But it is the likes of Stornaway she would be exposed to, you know, and he is not at all the thing."

"How did he look? Was he recovered from his accident?"

"He had one arm in a black sling, but told me it was a precaution only. He said he had written you at Alton's. I told him she was gone off to Bromley Hall. Servants are hopeless; they hadn't the wits to forward the letter here."

"Did he say he would come back?"

"No, my dear. You need not fear he will. I most particularly said he would not, to set your mind at rest."

Stark dismay overcame me. I could not conceal it, but its cause was misread by my cousin. Her mind was full of those two white cards, stuck into the mirror. "You are regretting the trip to the Pavilion," she told me. "How should it be possible to take Perdita there, and you? You have neither of you been presented . . . Of course it is a very informal do, not really any official residence either, only a holiday home. I think . . . ." She strode to the mirror and seized the cards. "Yes, it is a masquerade party, which is the very shabbiest sort of a do, but at least one's identity need not be known. We could take a quick peek in, just to see the place, and dart out

205

before the unmasking. It is a May Day party. To-morrow is the first of May. He will soon be going to London for the Season, I expect."

"Is it not the custom for the Prince to leave his party first, before the other guests depart?"

"I believe it is, but Stornaway mentioned twice its being only a small informal do. Of course he did not say so till I mentioned my disgust of big parties."

"It is too late to prepare costumes."

"Too late? Why, we would have all day tomorrow. Dominoes can be had ready-made, and masks . . ." I looked, to see whether to allow my hopes to soar once more, as they had when first she told me of the call. Her face was radiant. Though she did not realize it, the precious cards were held against her heart. "Since you are so eager to go, my dear, I shall oblige you in the matter. It will do Perdita a world of good to be on terms with the Prince when she goes to London, too. A little attention from him would set her up."

There was a small party coming in for dinner. The famous cards were removed from the mirror to sit on the sofa table, for easy discovery by the first lady who laid down her reticule. It chanced to be a Mrs. Carlisle.

"Maude—what is this?" she asked, picking them up. "How did the Prince ever hear of you?"

"Lord Stornaway, an acquaintance of my niece, called and brought the cards. The son of that shabby countess who billets herself at the Pavilion every spring."

"Ah, the handsome son! *That* explains it. He has Perdita in his eye. He flies too high for her, Maude. I saw Lady Stornaway in the royal carriage this afternoon. She is either the Prince's *chère amie* or the *chère amie*'s best friend. There is some uncertainty in the matter, but she is seen about *everywhere* with him. I would adore to meet her." Mrs. Carlisle received a half dozen glares at having let a piece of truth slip into her outpouring.

"She is lively, a pretty woman," one of the gentlemen was allowed to acknowledge.

"I saw her walking in the gardens in a damped gown, at *her* age," the admirer's spouse said spitefully.

"Wish *I* had seen her," the husband retaliated.

"You will never accept the invitation, Maude?" Mrs. Carlisle asked.

"Miss Greenwood has twisted my arm. She wants to go and see the Prince's treasures."

"What is the son like?" another lady asked.

"You must ask my niece," Maude replied, the interest of her caller mounting higher at every question and comment. "He was very taken with her. She has visited at his summer place, near Tunbridge Wells."

"I did not care for him," Perdita said firmly. "He is fast."

The neighbors nodded their heads in approval of her wisdom, and continued to proclaim their lack of interest in meeting such an infamous pair of rakes as the Stornaways for several minutes. Their indifference reached such heights they could speak of nothing else till dinner was served.

When the last hand of cards was played and the company departed, Maude said complacently that she had not had such a pleasant evening in years. Her only regret was that Gretta Norton had not been present.

"We shall go downtown very early in the morning to choose our dominoes and masks, to leave time to make a few preparations for the little party," she said casually.

We spent the better part of the next day making our "few preparations." The coiffeur was called in to construct an extravagant do for Maude, to curl Perdita's golden hair, and to arrange my own. We were all eager to check out the gown that would go

207

beneath the domino, to ensure that shoe buckles sparkled, that nails were manicured, that a strawberry or lemon facial was applied to fade any wayward spot, and bring a blush of healthy color. In short, the entire household was in a pucker throughout the whole day, running feverishly about borrowing nail trimmers, creams and pumice stones, darting to the shop for new silk stockings, for even the feet were to be done up in the highest kick of elegance.

Callers were turned from the door with no hardness of feelings. The Cosgrove set realized one did not to go to the Pavilion without twenty-four hours' hard preparing to appear natural. By the dinner hour, we were all tuckered out, and as fidgety as broody hens. Cook had prepared a special seafood dinner to honor the occasion. I hope it was enjoyed in the kitchen, for that is where three-quarters of it ended up.

As we arose from the table, three small corsages were brought to the door. "Roses," Mrs. Cosgrove said, smiling. "That was thoughtful of him." She held the card in her fingers. Her smile was not broad enough to indicate a princely sender.

"Who are they from?" I asked.

"Stornaway," she said, putting the card in her pocket. I was too shy to ask her to let me see it.

Chapter Twenty

At the appointed hour, we assembled in the saloon for a glass of sherry to reinforce us for the strain of making our curtsies to the Regent. With a final check in the mirror, we were off, rather wishing, at the last minute, that we had a male for escort. I don't believe a word was spoken between us as the carriage proceeded along the red-brick roadway of the Steyne, past the geometrical gardens, to the Pavilion Parade. We had not before entered into the private ten acres of ground, but had contented to drive past and look from the carriage.

The Pavilion was an impressive sight, its facade nearly five hundred feet long. One hardly knew what to feel, to look at the strange assortment of Moorish, Russian and Grecian architecture. Colonnade and entablature vied with green-roofed domes, minarets, cones and battlements. Bath stone and stuccoed brick and trellis-work jumbled together in pretty confusion.

"Barbaric!" Mrs. Cosgrove decreed happily.

"Oh I think it is *sweet!*" Perdita coo'd, while I found myself beyond not only speech, but even thought. I was a cauldron of turmoil that had nothing to do with the architecture. In a minute I would see him.

We entered the domed porch, to be shown through an octagonal vestibule with Chinese lanterns into a large hall, whose ceiling was painted like a cloud-laden sky. A last peek into the mirror over the marble mantel showed us three fearful faces. It also showed me what I never suspected before, that Aunt Maude rouged her cheeks. I wished I had done so. I looked too pale. A footman announced us, and we went into the Chinese Gallery.

We saw first-hand the First Gentleman of Europe, outfitted like the first dandy, in a gaudy white satin jacket, plastered with gold medals and ribbons. His portly frame was held into shape by a corset, whose stays creaked with the effort of containing such mountains of flesh. He was scented and powdered, and none too steady on his legs, though whether it were the drink or overweight that caused it was unclear. Both the light and the heat were over-whelming, like a desert at high noon, but a desert blooming with every manner of colorful, exotic flower.

We made our practiced curtsies, and were wel-comed most graciously to the Prince's little do. "I hope you will enjoy it. We don't see enough of the youngsters." Perdita was subjected to a covetous examination at this speech. "What is your name, lass?" he asked her.

"Perdita Brodie," she said shyly.

"Perdita! Ah, how it takes one back to his youth," he said, fingering a lace-edged handkerchief. "You are too young to be aware of Perdita and Florizel. Perhaps you, Mrs. Cosgrove, are familiar with that youthful, tragic tale."

She pulled a sympathetic face, though I had often heard her and her friends complain of his harsh treatment of his first mistress, Perdita Robinson.

"The wonderful folly of youth," he said, dabbing at

210

his rheumy eyes with the lace. "Take this beautiful lass away. I cannot bear the memories."

Before she obeyed the royal command, she found a moment to utter some phrases in praise of his building, and its treasures. They restored him to humor, before he turned to greet the next guests. Perdita was that easily forgotten. "John, you sly villain!" the Prince said jovially to some newcomer.

With our duty done, we were free to stare in open wonder at the scene around us. It was difficult to know whether we were in the orient, a hothouse, or a jewel shop-window. There was chinoiserie everywhere, there was the effigy of flowers on walls and forming lampshades, there was ironwork formed to resemble bamboo, and there was an opulence of gold and jewel tones that boggled the mind. Mirrors too abounded, to multiply the lights and ornaments and crowds out of all proportion. No elaborate masquerade costumes were in evidence. A dame or two had powdered her hair in the old style, while one gentleman wore a pink fitted coat and held a feathered hat that looked old and vaguely French. For the most part, the ladies wore very daring gowns, some of them damped to cling to figures that were either too portly or too meager to look well. The gentlemen wore black jackets, with a sprinkling of livelier colors.

We none of us recognized a single soul in the room. The guests were Londoners, famous personages from the nobility, politics and the sphere of arts, Maude told us, though she could not be sure which person represented which field. I personally could have been well entertained for a fortnight just looking at them. They were not beautiful, but they were interesting, in a dissipated way. They were also totally unimpressed with the Pavilion and the Prince.

"Oh well, if he is going to inflict his playing on us, I for one mean to retire with my dispatch box," one elderly gentleman said, and turned on his heel to slip out a side door.

The noise was at a high pitch. The ladies especially all talked at the top of their lungs on matters that ought to have been discussed in a whisper, or not at all. Snatches of indiscreet conversations floated on the air. ". . . said she was going to visit her mama, but went to stay the weekend with her lover at Hurley Hall . . .," "he felt obliged to call him out, but could not like to treat his wife's lover so shabby . . .," "lost ten thousand pounds at one sitting, and he owing every merchant in the city . . .," "saw him at the ball with Lord Peter's French whore, both of them disguised . . ." One speech in particular called my attention to the speaker. "If Sir Scawen thinks to make an honest woman of Lady Stornaway, I wish him luck of an impossible endeavor."

It was a gaunt, ugly woman in a hideous purple gown who spoke, to an even uglier man, who was wobbling on his feet. "Top of the trees, Nel . . ." was his incomprehensible reply. Then he turned and straggled away from the lady, to take another glass of wine from a servant. Strolling towards a table, he lifted a small gold box, a snuffbox I believe it was, and slipped it into his pocket. I could not but think of O'Reilly, and his light fingers. But he had at least the excuse of the shopkeeper's heavy thumb to justify his deed. The actresses too had penury to blame for their wanton carrying on. What excuse had these aristocrats, but boredom?

"It is *exactly* as I imagined," Maude said happily. "We really ought not to have come." She had no air of meaning to depart for all that.

It was impossible to disagree with her speech. There was not a person of character in the room. The gouty bodies and raddled faces of the guests spoke clearly of the dissipated life they led. Despite the grandeur, the wine and the noise, there was no real gaiety either, but only a desperate search for it. It was rather pitiful. Already, after only a quarter of an hour, the noise, the heat and the blazing lights were beginning to pall. Had it not been for Stornaway, I would have welcomed an excuse to leave. But I had come in hopes of seeing him, so set myself to the task of finding him out. He entered suddenly through one of the false bamboo arches, looking like a breath of spring, in all the surrounding decadence. I had not realized how well formed his body was, how tall and straight; his face too was at odds with the haggard countenances on all sides. His expression was alert, his eyes sparkling as he looked all around. When he spotted us, he advanced at a rapid gait, nearly capsizing an admiral in his haste.

He made a graceful bow, said his good evenings, and told Maude how happy he was that she had come. "I am not at all sure it was wise," she admitted, with a passing glance over the crowd.

"There is a quieter room with some card tables set up, if you would like to escape," he offered.

I do not think she had any real desire to escape, but to view another chamber was acceptable. We all went to a more sedate, though still gaudy, chamber where half a dozen tables were being made up. The misfits were assembled here, taking refuge from the din. A few Brighton acquaintances were discovered, and invited Maude to join them.

"I shall look after the ladies," Stornaway offered.

"We shall not stay long," Maude said aside to me. "No harm can come to you, though I dislike to think of you girls being exposed to those people. Keep a sharp eye on Perdita, my dear."

"There is some dancing going forth in the Crimson Saloon," he mentioned, as we left.

"Oh good! Let us go to the Crimson Saloon," Perdita said. "We shall never be back, and I would like to see as much as possible tonight."

The crowd here was younger than elsewhere. They were not yet so deeply sunk into dissipation as their

213

elders. Stornaway found a respectable gentleman friend in the throng who was very happy to be presented to Miss Brodie, and lead her to the floor.

"At last," he said, when we were alone.

He did not wear his black sling, but held the limb at a cautious angle, rather close against his body. "You are not able to dance yet. How is your wound, Stornaway? I hope you are recovering satisfactorily." I felt strangely shy, now that I was with him again.

"Is that all you have to say to me?" he asked, with a deprecatory shake of the head, as his fingers tightened on mine. "The wound is fine. I don't want to dance. We must find a quiet place to talk."

We walked to the edge of the room and sat on two highly original and uncomfortable chairs, that looked like tulips growing out of the floor. "Your aunt disapproves of me. Small wonder. She was barely civil when I called. I hoped she might succumb to the temptation of the Pavilion. I did not see how else I was to reach you, being hampered on all sides by propriety. Did she tell you I wrote you at Alton's, and the stupid servants did not forward the letter?"

"Yes, she told me." I noticed Stornaway was chattering in a nervous way, unlike himself.

"So what is to be done?" he asked bluntly.

"What do you mean?" I looked, trying to read his mind. It sounded ominously like a prelude to a brush-off. There was no smile, no intimacy in his words or tone.

"She has no actual authority over you, cannot forbid the match, or anything of that sort?"

My heart leapt for joy. "We have not spoken of a match, Stornaway," I mentioned. Forbid it, indeed! Much I cared if she forbid it a thousand times!

"You are having second thoughts," he said quietly. "This is not the optimum meeting place for me to convince you I am a reformed man. I am only here because of Mama, and because there was no room to be had at an inn, but mostly, of course, because *you* are at Brighton."

"I heard someone say your mother is to be married," I said, feeling some perverse urge to change the subject, to see how quickly he would return to it.

"Yes, the engagement is not formally announced yet. An old friend and neighbor, Sir Scawen Blinker, has offered for her. They have known each other anytime these thirty years. I could hardly be more surprised had she set up as a nun. About *us*, Molly. . ."

"Your mother is here, is she, at the Pavilion?"

"Yes, around somewhere. I'll present you to her later. Mol, stop diverting me. I'm a big boy. I can take it. You have changed your mind, is that it?" His eyes were brightly inquisitive, beautifully worried, as eager as a puppy's. "Rescue me," he said simply.

"A man must do that for himself."

"I am trying. Help me. I don't want to end up like these people. I thought I would, till I met you. I am convinced a marriage of convenience leads to nothing but—this," he flung his good arm out towards the dancers. "If a man is not happy at home, he leaves home as much as possible. And where does he go? Where his friends and acquaintances congregate —clubs, such dens as this. Stafford has already begun laying plans for the Season's dissipation, and he not married above a week. I had the most *pitiful* letter from him, trying to sound happy, you know . . . That is not going to happen to me. I am through with worldly-wise folly."

As he spoke, an elderly couple came into the room and sauntered towards us. The woman was pretty, rouged and carefully curled. The man at her side looked out of place, due to his austere expression and his sober outfit.

"Sonnie!" the lady chirped, holding her arms out to Stornaway. "Is this *her?*" she asked, looking towards me, her eyes widening.

I arose to greet the eldsters. "This is Miss Green-

wood, Mama, whom I have been telling you about."
They sat down with us. The mama subjected me to a
gentle quizzing, as any prospective mama-in-law
will do. I could not return the compliment, but no
questions were necessary to find her vain, silly, and
quite charming.

"I was in alt when I learned Sonnie had broken off
with that wretched Dulcinea," she said frankly. "The
duchess called, trying to patch it up, but I snubbed
her. It simply would not do. How could I have *borne*
to have her forever underfoot, disapproving of me?
He brought her home to me, you know, then *he*
slipped out early from the party and left me to
entertain her. It was the fear of her that nudged me
into accepting Scawen, but once it was done, I did
not back down, even though it was no longer necessary. Scawen disapproves of me too, but I can always
handle *him*."

Sir Scawen smiled so fatuously at this plain talking that there was no reason to doubt her. "I hear
you had a marvelous adventure with some actors.
You must tell me all about it. When you were
pointed out to me across the hall, I felt sure it was
the petite blonde Sonnie had fallen for. I am *so glad*
it was not. She don't look up to his weight, but I am
quite sure *you* could handle a whole herd of rakes,
my dear. You look very resolute."

"Oh! Thank you. I think?"

"I meant it as a compliment," she said, blinking
her great blue eyes at me.

They stayed for ten minutes talking to us. Sir
Scawen seemed a sensible man. Before leaving, he
told me he was vastly relieved to see Sonnie choose
so wisely. I hardly knew what he meant, but like the
mother's remark, it was meant for a compliment.

Stornaway never actually asked me in so many
words to marry him, so it was impossible to say yes.
Somehow, the news was known amongst those whose
business it was to be *au courant* with the latest

gossip. The ugly lady in purple I had overheard earlier came prancing up to us. She was introduced by Stornaway as the Russian ambassador's wife, the Countess Lieven, a social lioness.

"Which of you is Stornaway's young lady?" she demanded. Perdita sat with us at the time. "It must be you, Miss Greenwood. He keeps ranting on about emerald eyes, so it cannot be this blonde. My congratulations upon weaning him away from Sarnia's gel. She has got all the liveliness of a garden slug, and the same complexion too, muddy pink. You look a sensible dame. Tether him tight, but not too tight."

"Hush, milady," Stornaway said, teasing her.

"What a brash fellow it is, but we will always take commands from a handsome young fellow, if only he will tease us a little."

"I don't want you giving Miss Greenwood the notion I am not to be trusted."

"Rubbish! Who wants a man she can trust, eh, Miss Greenwood? I would as lief trust Stornaway with a woman as I would an eagle in a dovecote. But he ain't *all* bad. He is amusing, at least. The Prince has been prosing on till my ears hum about his new diet, or maybe it was some book he is trying to read. I fell asleep with my eyes open. A trick we ambassadors' wives learn early on in the game. It would take an insomniac to hear him to the end without a snooze. He sets us all to snoring. It is only your mama's damped gowns that keep the gentlemen awake these evenings, Stornaway. She'll take rheumatism, certainly, and has grown too stout to look well in the latest craze, too, but she ain't quite a caricature yet."

"She will be flattered to hear it, ma'am."

"Devil a bit of it. She'll scratch my eyes out. It is true for all that. They are saying she plans to marry Blinker. *Tell* me it is all a hum!"

"No, it is true."

"The best joke I have heard all night. 'Twill be the

217

makings of her. He'll preach her into propriety, or she will smile him into fashion. We shall see who is the stronger. My money is on Sir Scawen. I must run and hide. Here comes Prinney, with another old *on-dit* or new diet to pester me with. We shall see you at Almack's, I hope?"

She was gone, with the portly Prince in hot pursuit.

Aunt Maude was in no hurry to leave the Pavilion, once she got out of the card room and into the thick of the infamy. Even after the Prince departed, our party was by no means the first to leave. Stornaway buttered Maude up as best he could by being polite to her, getting her a tray of food, and keeping the more reprehensible company at bay. The last effort was by no means appreciated.

"May I call on you tomorrow, ma'am?" he asked, as we stood awaiting our carriage.

It was difficult to say no, after having accepted half an hour's courtesy from him. She agreed, with no lack of enthusiasm. I tried to give her some inkling of his errand, as we drove home, by pointing out his superiority to the others encountered that evening, and how well it would be for him to be removed from that set. But she was paying me little heed, so at last I just blurted it out.

"Marriage? Are you sure it is marriage he has in mind, Moira?" she asked.

"Quite sure."

"Pray do not feel you must have him. I will always be happy for your company."

"I want to marry him."

I could not see, in the darkness of the carriage, but felt she was staring at me. "His mama's such a scatterbrain!" she exclaimed, for she had been presented to the countess. "But Sir Scawen at least seemed a decent man," was the nature of her congratulations to me.

Perdita was hardly more enthusiastic. "You mustn't!" was her advice.

"Why, you always spoke of the felicity of taming a rake," I reminded her.

"Yes, but I didn't know what I was talking about then. So you will be a countess, Moira?" she said a moment later, a little piqued. I knew what her expression was too. Petulant, the chin up.

"Yes, shocking, is it not?"

"It is unbelievable. I daresay *I* may look forward to marrying a duke, when I am presented."

"I don't see why not."

"We shall see a good deal of each other in London," Aunt Maude said, quite happily. "*He* will not take up much of your time. I know how his sort go on, but of course it is a match with much to recommend it. A lady in your position is not looking for a *love* match. You must introduce us to all the fine gentlemen, Moira. My, princes and countesses, what a night it has been! The Prince so very taken with you, Perdita. There was a tear in his eye. I met two ambassadors and a Cabinet minister's wife. There is something to be said for the Prince's Pavilion after all, though he keeps it too hot by far."

"I nearly fainted," Perdita said, with a yawn.

"The Cabinet minister's wife said she would call on us tomorrow," Maude continued happily.

"I danced with a baron," Perdita said.

"I wonder if she will bring her husband with her. She mentioned the countess might come. What ought one to serve a countess to drink or eat, Moira?"

"I don't know. I have not learned the rules yet," I replied.

Aunt Maude continued to comment in a blatantly impressed manner about the social conquests she had made; Perdita answered quite at random with conquests of her own, and I sat like a cat in the cream, smiling softly in the darkness, knowing I had made the best success of all.

Chapter Twenty-one

When Stornaway came to call next morning, Aunt Maude already had her saloon cluttered up with the Cabinet minister's wife and one countess. I sat awaiting Stornaway in the study. He asked my cousin, between the hall and the study, whether she had any objection to the match, and if he is to be believed, she asked *him* what she ought to serve her guests. She told him with some alacrity that she would be happy to have him for a connection, while he told her that Lady Hetherston, he believed, liked tea and biscuits on a morning call, whereas the Cabinet minister's wife was said to have no objection to a glass of wine at any time of day, but after dinner she preferred brandy.

"Thank God she came in the morning! I have not a drop of brandy in the house. Where should I get some?" she said, standing in a fit of abstraction at the door, till she remembered why her latest guest had come. She said, "I suppose you will want this door closed," before walking away and leaving it wide open.

Stornaway looked after her. He closed the door

and advanced to the sofa where I sat, trembling like a blancmange.

"I wish I had someone to advise me on the proper procedure expected of me. Do I go down on my knees, or what?" he asked uncertainly.

"I cannot help you. This is my first time."

"I feel I should be grovelling on all fours."

"Three will be enough. We don't want to subject your clipped wing to such harsh usage."

"You are a world too good for me." He sat beside me, and smiled rather shyly. "You know why I am here. After rehearsing half the night, I have forgotten my lines. Miss Greenwood," he said, straightening his shoulders, "I am come to ask if you will do me the honor . . . that is . . . I know I am not at all . . . I have no right to expect . . . Oh damme, Molly, will you marry me?"

I was better prepared. "Yes," I said, loud and clear.

"You won't be sorry. You won't ever be sorry. I am going to make you the best husband you ever had."

Foolishness is easily forgiven an ardent lover, especially when his actions are so much more speaking than his words. There was none of that tentative quality in his embrace. It was exquisitely appropriate to the occasion—tender, yet not without passion. In fact, with so much of passion that I feared for his recovering wound, and my own sanity. I felt deliriously happy. "I mean to be a good wife too, Storn," I said, when I had the opportunity.

"You couldn't be a bad one if you tried, Molly. Moira—I love you both." He kissed my nose, and both eyes.

"I was rather fond of Mr. Brown, too."

"He is at your disposal, any time you feel the urge for a change of partner."

"I won't feel any such urge for a long, long time."

Perdita had the first word, and she shall have the last, as she chose that inopportune moment to invade our privacy. She had come to read him a lecture, if you please, to issue some dire and mostly incomprehensible threats regarding what she would do if I were mistreated.

"Miss Greenwood is not without friends, friends in high places," she warned. "If I ever hear of your abusing her *in any way,* Lord Stornaway, you may expect to deal with *me.*"

"Sufficient threat to tame a tiger. I would not deal with you again for any consideration."

She looked, wondering if this was a compliment. "You are always welcome back as my chaperone, Moira," she added, with a wonderfully noble countenance, the one usually reserved for high heroism in the dramatic academy. With just such a raised chin did Cordelia proclaim her love for King Lear, according to her duty.

"You are very kind," I said, trying to keep my voice steady.

"I know it."

"Also very much *de trop,*" Stornaway told her, arising to show her the door.

"I shall be right outside, if you need me," was her parting speech.

He drew out his handkerchief, stuck the end of it into the keyhole, and turned back to me, with an anticipatory smile on his face. "Now, Molly, where were we?"

Let COVENTRY Give You
A Little Old-Fashioned Romance

☐	**LADY BRANDY** by Claudette Williams	50165	$1.75
☐	**THE SWANS OF BRHYADR** by Vivienne Couldrey	50166	$1.75
☐	**HONORA CLARE** by Sheila Bishop	50167	$1.75
☐	**TWIST OF CHANCE** by Elisabeth Carey	50169	$1.75
☐	**THE RELUCTANT RIVALS** by Georgina Grey	50170	$1.75
☐	**THE MERCHANT'S DAUGHTER** by Rachelle Edwards	50172	$1.75

Buy them at your local bookstore or use this handy coupon for ordering.

COLUMBIA BOOK SERVICE (a CBS Publications Co.)
32275 Mally Road, P.O. Box FB, Madison Heights, MI 48071

Please send me the books I have checked above. Orders for less than 5 books must include 75¢ for the first book and 25¢ for each additional book to cover postage and handling. Orders for 5 books or more postage is FREE. Send check or money order only.

Cost $_____ Name _____

Sales tax*_____ Address _____

Postage_____ City _____

Total $_____ State _____ Zip _____

The government requires us to collect sales tax in all states except AK, DE, MT, NH and OR.

This offer expires 1 December 81   8136